THE SIEGE OF TRAPP'S MILL

Annabel Farjeon

THE SIEGE OF TRAPP'S MILL

Atheneum 1974 New York

Library of Congress catalog card number 73-84826
ISBN 0-689-30136-7
Published simultaneously in Canada by
McClelland & Stewart, Ltd.
Manufactured in the United States of America by
Halliday Lithograph Corporation
West Hanover, Massachusetts
First Atheneum Edition

THE
SIEGE OF
TRAPP'S
MILL

1

It was winter and very cold. The sky was an even grey colour that pressed lower and lower over the town of Slidden as Friday evening drew on.

At this time certain boys collected in the Trapp, an empty mill that for a hundred years had spun yarn and now stood derelict. It lay on rising ground overlooking a waste country-side, where mining had left heaps of slag: black pyramids, large and small, on which no plant would grow the grit was so acid. Between these a scrub of coarse grass, thistle and sorrel struggled for life. Now and then sheep would stray in from the moor beyond and lose their way in the maze of hillocks. This was dangerous, for there were overgrown, for-gotten shafts into which they sometimes tumbled.

Standing lonely, the mill had been built of pale solid stone, but this had become coloured by smoke and was now deep ingrained black. It was two storeys high and, from a distance, appeared as firm and grim as a castle, with the half-broken chimney stack like a turret at one end. The window glass was almost all smashed, but thick iron frames had stood up to the local lads and kept them out, only rusting orange and flaking away as the years of neglect in-creased.

Now at last boys had found a way in. They came at the

weekend or after school to escape from their homes, where the small rooms were cluttered with furniture, with brothers and sisters, with nagging parents and the uncontrollable telly.

At four-thirty on this Friday afternoon in January there were three of them: Polak, Shem and Es. It was they who had broken in a month ago, and it was they who came most regularly at weekends to feed Fleabag. Fleabag was an enormous mottled cat, with a short bushy tail and sharp-looking face, that seemed to have been pressed back and flattened. His ears were torn with fighting, his coat was a yellowish sandy grey, with dark streaks over the back and round the tail. Fleas inhabited his fur. It was unwise to touch him, both because of the insects and because, unless he gave permission, he might stab with terrible claws and then back away hissing and bristling. More than one boy had been wounded. He was protected as far as possible from retaliatory kicks by little Es, who maintained that the Trapp was under the cat's guardianship.

'It's him as lives here all the year round. It's him as stops the rats taking over. He's caretaker.'

Polak said: 'Nay, he's boss. He gives parties for his friends in the shop when it's full moon. I wouldn't take liberties with that cat. It's Fleabag's place.'

'I got some animal mince from Frank Hall. He says you get more goodness out of meat than those fish pieces—more blood!' Es gloated, holding up a soggy, brown-stained parcel of newspaper. 'That's three penn'orth.'

They were standing in the lavatory, where they had entered via the barred window. Es could squeeze through easily enough: he was the youngest and small for twelve; but Shem, who was tall and lanky and fourteen, had stuck half way today, his body balanced like a seesaw. He had panicked.

'I'll never do it! I'm jammed! You'll have to saw through

6

them bars to get me out. I can feel my belly swelling—I can't move! You'll have to call the fire brigade——'

'Don't kick me in the face, you!' Polak called from outside, where legs dangled in the air. 'Hang onto his shoulders, Es, and I'll push. Don't stiffen—let go!'

Inside Es held the floundering top half as best he could, while Polak pushed. Slowly, like an awkward parcel, Shem subsided to the slate floor, head first, complaining as he crushed Es beneath him.

'There, see? You can do it if you try. I told you so. Didn't I tell you? Only wish I was a midget like you, Es. You aren't half lucky.'

Es pushed him off and punched him in a conventional gesture of defiance.

Then they looked up to see Polak's projecting face. His shoulders were edging and struggling sideways after the head, one of his hands pressed down the wall, the other gripped the sill. Although Polak was thicker built than Shem, he was far more agile; but he too seemed to stick half way. He did not panic, only his cheeks, forehead and neck turned red and white in blotches that appeared bright against his pale hay-coloured hair. He gasped with shallow breaths.

'This floor is cold as hell,' Shem said, stumbling to his feet.

Polak retorted in a strangled voice: 'Hell is hot.'

With a jerk he pulled his hips and dived. Es and Shem caught the heavy shoulders as he came thudding down, clutching at Es's yellow curls.

'Look out for my baked beans!' Es cried, snatching at his carrier bag too late. It ripped.

'You'll have to let the rope down next time, Esmond Cattermole. We've grown too fat.' Polak spoke certain words with a curious vibrating accent, for although he had been born in the district, they spoke Polish at home. His parents had been war-time refugees.

Shem led the way along the corridor chanting:

'Penny for the cat!
Penny for the cat!
Put it in a hat,
Penny for the cat!'

'Snow's coming. Can't you smell it?' Es remarked, clutching the carrier to his chest. 'You'll have to give me three pence this time—unless the others turn up. I brought a tin of baked beans, some milk and a bit of tea I nicked off Mum.'

His shrill voice echoed as they came to the high stair-well that led up to the store-room on the first floor. The vast workshop below, whose door stood open, was littered with the remains of the great clearance when the machinery had been sold for scrap. There was straw, a long broken pulley belt, iron bolts projecting from the wall and a pile of scaffold poles that had been brought up and left at a time when it was thought the stack might be repaired. Only the straw was useful to start fires in the store-room above.

'Not many won't come if it snows,' Shem said, glancing into the workshop, through whose windows the wind whistled.

Es brushed past him and went into a dark dank office at the back. He thrust his arm up the chimney: there was the slither and rattle of falling soot as he brought out a rusty saw hidden there. In the corner of this room stood a high, old-fashioned desk. Es went up to it and wrenched back the lid.

'Anyway we're going to have a decent blaze tonight,' he said. 'Not like last time. I'm not freezing for anyone.' He tugged again, in a hurry.

'Hey,' Polak cried from the doorway, 'you want to cut off legs, that's all. We could use the top for sitting on.'

Es immediately let the lid drop and began to saw sideways at a leg with small violent pushes.

'This saw's bloody blunt! You two go on up with the nosh and I'll bring wood. These legs'll burn lovely.'

8

'Don't force her—let her run easy,' Polak advised as the saw jammed. 'You'd do better if you laid it on one side.'

'Aw shut up telling me!' Es exclaimed.

However, when he heard them mount the stair he pushed the desk, which fell over with a satisfying crash. He sawed off the legs about three inches from the top and the cross-bars fell out of their own accord. When he set the desk upright it wobbled on its stumps.

Something clattered within, so he opened the lid to find a dried-up bottle of Stephens ink, rolled to the front. As he took hold an enormous black spider ran out of the mouth and raced to the recess at the back. Es dropped the bottle with a squeak and more cautiously retrieved a long narrow account book. The pages were ruled, red lines down and blue lines across. The black cover was spotted with mould.

Es carried the sticks to the store-room where Polak was rolling sheets of newspaper diagonally on the floor. He spread each page flat, licked the corner with his short round tongue and then flicked the wet piece between his thumb and first finger. The paper curled over like the tight frond of a fern and the roll grew longer and longer as he pushed it against the boards. When the sheet had become a thin rod, he bent it round and tied a knot.

'There's a lovely one,' he said, holding up a hard smooth spear of paper.

'Don't bend it. Let's fight—they're good for swords,' Es cried, dropping his sticks.

They stood opposite each other, sideways, the back arm raised, like fencers they had seen on the TV. They bent one knee, crossed their paper swords and tapped them together.

'On guard!'

'Counter cut!'

'*Touché!*'

'No you didn't!'

'Lunge!'

9

The swords smacked together and Polak's drooped, a broken reed. Es, excited, slashed with the tip of his own, which snapped off and fell to the floor. They stood laughing and heard Shem call.

'Oi! You two—come in here!'

Shem was in the room which had been built above the downstairs office. It was the same size, only here the glass of the window was intact, misted over with cobwebs that thickened at each corner. There was a grate with a slate mantelpiece. Shem was straddling on the broken brown linoleum that still covered parts of the floor, when Es arrived.

'I've an idea! We'll move in. We'll light the fire. Panes aren't even cracked.' He tossed back the lank hair that was always falling across his eyes, thrust out his long hollow jaw and clapped his hands, then rubbed them together. 'Might even get warm. Might even.' His face was gay and crinkled, his limbs moved jerkily.

'Aye—let's ask Polak.'

'Ask Polak!' Shem was quickly irritated. 'We don't have to ask Sir Polak's permission for everything.'

Es hurriedly changed his tactics. 'We could fetch that desk up to sit on. We could cook. Look at them thick bars.' He kicked the grate with his black boot and rust fell.

Shem stroked his jaw bone feeling for hair. 'Get on with it then. Fetch in the gear. This is a place. It's that posh you might call it the front room.'

2

The three boys were crouching round the blazing desk legs when Shem heard a shout. He pushed his chin forward, put his head on one side and frowned.

'That's them.'

'You sure? I didn't hear nothing,' Es said.

'Then you go and see,' Shem ordered.

Es gave a quick look at Polak. He was afraid to go alone, yet dared not disobey. Polak understood the appeal and would not respond. After a moment's hesitation Es rose. Light was fading, a whitish blur of snow raced past the window. Outside the corridor was dim. Es tensed his body against fear and walked on. All sounds were dominated by the whining wind.

In the store-room a newspaper sheet, left there by Polak, was gently shifting itself across the floor, lifted spasmodically by the draught and whispering as it went. It was icy cold and on the boards beneath each of the eight windows, eight mounds of snow shone white.

A ragged figure was standing outside in the flurry, its mouth wide open, shouting, shouting. Polak came to stand beside Es and together they yelled back, putting their arms out between the iron frame to wave. But the gale swept their voices away and the snow masked their signals. The boy below could not see or hear them.

At the far end of this room were two heavy wooden doors. These led onto a small open-air platform, above which hung a pulley and a rope. In the old days this had been used to haul up bales of wool, fresh cut from the moorland sheep. Now it was employed in drawing up any boy who was too big to squeeze through the lavatory window. The more agile ones could climb the rope by themselves.

Polak let the rope down. The rusted pulley wheel squeaked as the rope moved over the groove and flopped onto the snow. At the same time Es banged the wooden doors with an empty oil can, and this clanging at length attracted the newcomer's attention. He ran round the corner of the building, looked up and waved, then stepped onto the knotted end of the rope, holding it with both arms stretched above his head.

Es now called Shem and they set to work turning the handle of the wheel that drew up the rope. It was hard going. The boy swung about in mid air, with great flakes flying at him like a horde of onrushing locusts. The hands of the haulers grew hot and sore. Es had little strength and was mostly used to belay the rope on an iron hook that projected from the wall or to report on progress, which he did with yelps of excitement. Polak gave orders and took the chief strain, for he was strong, with a square back, thick wrists and the knees of a footballer. His hair stood in an unruly brush, his grey eyes stared with the desperate effort.

Shem complained in a stream of despair. 'Ee—my back! This'll be the death of me. There's a blister on my hand the size of an egg. Tell him to stop wriggling, Es. Go on, tell him to jump off or I'll let go.'

With a rest half way, they dragged the boy in. It was George, a sad-eyed, tattered fellow with a goggling Adam's apple, whose clothes included a neat pinstripe waistcoat, which he had lately bought with his own money second hand. He was proud of this, his only decent garment, but had been much laughed at in school. When at length he scrambled over the platform and stood upright in the dim light, they saw that under his old jacket the waistcoat hung open and he was shivering violently.

'You come on in to our front room,' Es invited him. 'We've a smashing fire.'

Polak stood staring at the whiteness. Through the maze of snow the outline of the moor could no longer be seen. Then he closed the doors with a clang and shot the bolts.

George kicked petulantly at a pile of snow under the window and peered out.

'They may be coming,' he said in his husky voice. 'They're after me.'

'Who—Bullman lads?' Shem demanded.

'They followed me up the dump. I tried to throw them off, but they guessed I was coming here. It was six to one.'

Es came to the window too, but the flakes fell so thick he could not see the ground.

In the front room George went straight to the fire, rubbing his red and blue hands. When they were all gathered he stepped back, standing straight, and exclaimed: 'And they got me. See what they done!'

His friends looked for some sign of injury, for blood, a black eye, torn clothing. But there was the same old grey shirt bulging out below the waistcoat and the familiar piece of postman's string holding up his uncle's discarded trousers.

Es demanded in high voice: 'How do you mean? I can't see nothing.'

'Can't see?' George's voice rose. 'Can't see? Can't you see they cut off my waistcoat buttons?' His face grimaced in the firelight, agonized. For a moment it seemed as though he would burst into tears.

Immediately they understood why the garment hung open.

Es came close to inspect. 'Aye, they have and all!'

13

Shem burst out laughing, Es giggled. But Polak pulled down the corners of his shapely mouth and raised his splayed nostrils with a sardonic expression of anger.

'I knew you'd just laugh,' George said bitterly.

Shem doubled up and sat on the desk. 'Poor old George!' he gasped. 'Lost all your buttons!' He gave a falsetto shriek.

'I'm not laughing,' Polak said.

Now Es checked himself, seeing that Polak did not think it funny. 'If they come, there's six.'

'And here's three and a bit,' Polak muttered, considering his own forces. 'How many of them are small enough to get in the bog window, eh George?'

'Four at least,' George replied. 'There was Norman and Al and the twins—they could. And Fordyce and Red. It was Red that done it.'

Shem stopped laughing. 'Let's get organized, lads. You'd best go and barricade that window. I'll start cooking. And bring up any wood you can scrounge. See what we got here, George, baked beans!' He held up the tin.

It was accepted that Shem cooked, for he intended to take up catering when he left school.

George glanced aside quickly, lest the sight of the tin should subdue his indignation.

'You can laugh,' he muttered angrily.

Es laid his hand on George's shoulder. 'You stay here and get yourself warm. Polak and me'll fix the window, won't we?'

His voice and hand were gentle, his face under the tousled curls so appealing that tension relaxed, and although George replied with obstinate determination, they all knew that this was a formality, that the words were a few steps before the return of good humour.

'Nay, I'm coming.'

And he gave Shem a sullen stare, just to show he was not forgiving him too quickly.

14

The wind outside stirred to a long thin whistle, wavering up and down. The chimney gave a belch of smoke. No one wanted to leave the fire that scorched their faces and made them cough so comfortingly.

'Come on, lads,' said Polak. 'Must be done.'

'I'll never find them again on the dump—with this snow and all,' George moaned.

Es cried: 'Who wants to find that lot? I'd rather keep out of their way, thank you!'

Polak smiled at George, understanding. 'Nay, lad, I doubt you'll find them again. But don't fret, there's buttons enough in the world to go round.'

3

It was more difficult to barricade the lavatory window than they anticipated. They dragged in scaffold poles from the pile on the workshop floor and tried to wedge these against the bars and across the stalls. But, as Polak pointed out, it would not take much force to dislodge them. Feet ached with cold, fingers grew stiff and clumsy on the freezing metal and they longed to be back in their front room with the scent of baked beans rising. Only fear of those outside whispering voices, and the panic sensation knowing 'It's them—the Bullman gang!' kept the boys struggling with unwieldy lengths of steel, clashing along the corridor, jamming round the corner.

Twice Es remarked: 'This snow'll set them back a bit. They'll never bother,' hoping thereby to discourage his elders from further effort.

They went on in the fading light until the tangle must at least hold up intruders. But it was an ill-managed confusion that chiefly expressed fear of the enemy.

They returned, carrying a big packing case to serve as another seat, and there, sure enough, came the smell of baked beans, hot bubbles round the edge of the tin precariously balanced in the grate, and Shem complaining.

'Come on, come on! Your dinner's been spoiling this half-hour. I don't know what things are coming to—you treat this place like an hotel. No consideration for mother at all! I hope you washed your hands. No dinner till I've passed your fingernails!'

He lifted the can out between two sticks and set it in the middle of the floor. The crooked spoon, one of their prized possessions, looked as though it was bending under the delicious weight of beans. Es perched on the packing case, his legs dangling, Polak sat on the desk, Shem squatted low on an oil drum, George leant against the mantelpiece, raising one foot after the other to the heat, so that his boots steamed in turn.

'My go!' cried George, stretching his chilblained fingers for the spoon.

'Don't drop it—tin's hot,' said Es.

Their faces burned, their backs froze.

'You made tea?' Polak asked.

'Kettle's on the boil,' Shem replied.

The kettle was huge and battered. It leaked under the spout, so that if filled above this level water oozed and sizzled slowly on the black outside. They had also a brown teapot with its spout snapped off half way and a blue willow-pattern lid. There was one mug without a handle, which Shem had filched from the back of his mother's cupboard.

'If only we could live here,' sighed little Es, watching Shem heat the teapot and then fling the water away onto the floor behind him.

'Ee! don't waste that!' shouted George in a husky falsetto.

The weekend before he had filled the kettle from an outside tap that still flowed. This was the remainder of the water.

'Don't fret, we can melt snow,' Polak said.

So he took the empty kettle and went in search of snow.

'Shut the door!' they yelled in unison, as an icy blast swept in.

It was pitch black in the corridor and Polak had to feel

his way along the wall till he passed the stair and found the store-room door. Moving blindly he grew nervous, his ears alert for some sound of 'them', the enemy who had been so completely forgotten in the safe warmth of the front room. His knee banged sharply against an empty oil drum and its clang resounded like a gong through the hall, making him stop and hold his breath at the unexpected sensation of pain. Then he heard the screech, a long rise and fall of sound rasping through the air.

He stood aghast, till panic seized him lest the sound had come not from outside, but from the hall immediately below. He fumbled for the door handle, which took time to find and turn, and then a weight seemed to push, as though someone was pressing from the other side. As soon as the door came half open a blast of wind struck, so that he must lean forward to remain on balance.

Under each window the mounds of white had grown: they glowed with a ghostly pallor in the lesser darkness of the great store-room. Stiff with fear, Polak went to look out, but nothing could be seen. So he began scooping the snow in cupped hands and stuffing it into the kettle. When it was crammed full he straightened and began to sing loudly:

'Wojenko, wojenko, co jest ta za pani?
Ida za toba chlopce malovane,
Chlopce malowane sami wybierane.
Wojenko, wojenko, co jest ta za pani?'

The song gave him courage to go back along the corridor, for the thought of the hollow stairway chilled his blood: anything might rush up out of that pit of seething blackness. His aunt's tales of witches and werewolves in dark pine forests came to mind. He stopped and listened for the scream. The hall was alive with swishing and creaking and whistling. Gripping the kettle hard and humming between clenched teeth, Polak crossed the abyss and re-entered the front room.

Fire blazed, lighting the young faces a pinky orange, while their bodies sank away into darkness. Black shade filled all the outer room. Shem had laid a wooden ball, that once decorated the bottom of the stair balustrade, in the grate. On one side it glowed red hot, on the other the varnish ruckled, and bubbled a rich brown treacle.

'Pity you burnt that,' Es said. 'We could have played a game of football.'

'There's one on the other post,' Shem replied.

'Did you hear it?' Polak demanded.

'What?'

'Hear what?'

Polak said no more, but settled the kettle on the fire.

Shem continued his previous conversation with George. 'You know what it is? The problem with living with your own family is that you can't keep out unsavoury types. You've got to face it. I mean, some are all right, but others— you wouldn't be seen dead with—not if you could help it. I don't hold with relatives. I believe in good friends: they aren't forced down your throat, like crappy old aunts and things. Friends are what you choose.'

Es and Polak, stout family boys, were too shocked to object.

George said gloomily: 'Look at my Mum, she always says she wouldn't never have married, not if she'd known. Of course, she's not now, but what she's got's no better.'

'You can't always blame women,' Shem said. 'Look at my big sister, Rose. There she is slaving day and night for her old man and the kids. He has his forty-hour week and then puts his feet up. Won't lift a finger, not even carrying coals. I'd give him feet up, if I was six foot three!'

'That's what women—that's women's job,' said Polak. 'That's what they're made for—for kids and housework.'

Es nodded his curly head eagerly. 'That's right.'

George stood up, he was indignant. 'What do you mean—

that's what they're made for? Who says? Are you God Almighty to decide? You're just talking like an old grand-mother.'

Es piped: 'We men can't have the babies, can we?'

'So what, lad? When they're all born in test tubes what then? And look at the lasses that work full time, just like men! And on top of that they do all the cooking and babies and washing. You'd go back to the days of slavery if you could, wouldn't you, Polak? Women down the pits pulling the trucks, eh?'

Polak flushed with anger and a sense of frustration. 'Nay, that's what you want. I say women are best cooking back in the house.'

Shem said: 'I don't hold with females getting above them-selves.'

George interrupted. 'What I say is, women might even be better at being prime minister and all, give them half a chance. But they've been kept under for millions of years and there's not much—not much initiative as you might say left in them. As for being best at babies, I believe we could make a better job of that and all.' He grinned. 'Not that I hold with females——'

Es stuttered: 'Then—then what—what—what are you standing up for them for?'

'I stand up for justice.'

Polak spoke slowly. 'I do not think it has worked out this way for no reason—and—and——' He dropped his head sideways and rubbed his ear on his shoulder. 'Anyway, I think to have all those different people in a family—not only the ones you choose—I think it is meant to teach you under-standing.'

'Who says what was meant? And whatever—whatever—you're asking too much of human nature,' George responded derisively. 'Understanding—wow!'

Es was worried by George's sarcasm, frightened that his

friends would fall out and never make it up. He jumped down, his forehead wrinkled, and poked a piece of wood at the fire. 'Go on, Shem, make another brew. Kettle's boiling.'

'Stop mucking up my fire!'

'No one's paid Es his money yet,' Polak said, taking some coins from his pocket.

Shem poured sizzling, dripping water from the kettle into the teapot.

'Sssh! Listen!' Es gasped.

There was a faint scraping sound outside the door and they all shifted to see. In the dim light the blackened brass handle began to turn. It turned and turned and then, with a click and rattle, the latch slipped back into its socket. Firelight flickered on the door, which remained closed.

The four boys did not move.

Again there was a rasp and the handle began to turn, but just as the door seemed about to open, the knob reversed and the latch shot back.

There was silence.

Es spoke stiffly. 'It's a spook. I know it is!'

They considered this idea.

'Nay,' George whispered. 'It's them—the Bullman gang, trying to scare us.'

He was so obviously scared himself that Shem was roused. 'Looks like they succeeded. Looks like they——'

The handle began to move once more and Es let out a small gulp of terror, his face white.

With a sudden leap Polak went striding across the room. He took a firm hold of the knob and pulled, crying fiercely: 'Come in, you devils!'

There was a hiss from the darkness. Polak peered and, with a cry of surprise, burst out laughing. His face flooded pink.

Shem and George went over. Only Es remained unable to move, his hands clutching the edge of the packing case.

Shem cried irritably: 'What's the joke?'

Slowly, with tail erect, a large brindled cat stalked in.

Es let out his breath. Shem and George laughed.

'Shut the door!' Shem gasped. 'Draught's enough to cut your knees off.'

Es was poking in the carrier bag, while the cat rubbed against his leg, kneading the floor and purring.

'You devil! You clever old Fleabag!' Es kept exclaiming affectionately.

'Come on, lads, we owe Es for the nosh.'

'Not so good when only a few of us turn up,' Shem commented. 'I'm skint.'

Polak stood before them, his right fist raised, his left palm extended. 'Pay up! Three pence apiece.'

They paid and drank more tea, passing the mug from one to another and sipping, and making themselves burp, and laughing noisily.

4

Climbing out of the Trapp in the dark took even longer than climbing in, because of the barricade and George's awkwardness. It would have been quicker had three of them slid down the rope, while the fourth pulled it back and then squeezed through the window. But they thought of this too late.

George slipped and twisted his knee when he failed to get a proper grip on the window frame. He fell among crisscross rods and sat there groaning, until they threatened to leave him for the night. He limped all the way back.

Outside the sky had cleared. The snow was not deep, but light and crisp on the frozen earth. They kicked it up in a glistening froth as they tramped.

'I expect this is what Switzerland is like,' Es said.

Polak stopped whistling and gazed up at the star-speckled sky. 'This is how is my home. Beautiful.'

'Your home?'

'My home is Poland.'

'Yah!' Shem jeered. And then: 'Ow!'

For Polak had hit him in the ribs. He slithered across the path into a drift that disguised the height of a towering hedge, itself covered with snow. As he hit the bank and staggered to keep his feet, there was a soft, growing rustle; then snow showered over in a huge white eiderdown and the boy disappeared. The next minute he emerged with flaying arms, shouting, while the others rocked with laughter. George hopped on his good leg and coughed and choked and giggled.

Es turned to stare at George. 'And you don't half look like a scarecrow.'

George limped forward, stiff with indignation.

'Hey, come on, Georgey luv!' Shem shouted, stepping out of the snow and putting his arm over the thin shoulders. 'I don't sulk at Polak, even though he did punch me up the stomach.' Shem knew from experience that once George felt himself insulted there was no telling when he would get over it.

George glared at Es, who had slunk beside Polak. He spoke with a husky sob that came readily to his voice and drove certain boys to bully him. 'Right, young Esmond! Right! Next time you just remember blokes like me won't stand for being called a scarecrow. It's no joke, being me.'

They considered George's home life in silence. How his father had been killed in a pit accident; how his uncle knocked him about; the haggard look on his mother's face as she opened the front door with a mauvy-white baby in her arms. They knew he came to school hungry in the morning; they knew his bronchitis made the breath squeak in his chest.

'What you need is some decent place to live,' Polak said. 'One of them hostels or something. Suppose you talk to old Mac?'

Old Mac was headmaster of their secondary school.

George gave a bitter snort. 'Look, mate, I'm not fourteen yet. What can old Mac do? Anyway it's only Friday and Saturday nights I need to be away from the place—from him.' Friday and Saturday were pub nights for George's uncle. He continued wistfully: 'Wouldn't it be great to spend Saturday night in the Trapp?' He stopped and held onto the first lamp-post that marked the beginning of

Slidden. He lifted his aching leg out of the snow, coughed and spat neatly at the notice that read 'Road liable to subsidence'.

Es cried with an enthusiasm that was partly forced by a desire to placate George: 'That'd be smashing! Why not all of us?' He kicked up one foot after the other.

Polak brushed snow off Shem's shoulder. 'Maybe they wouldn't let us.'

Es immediately stopped jigging and echoed sadly: 'Nay, mine wouldn't.'

Shem lifted an arm to command attention. 'Listen, lads —now listen! Supposing I says to my Dad: "Saturday night I'm going to stay up at George's place." And then George says to his Mum: "Saturday night Shem asked me to stay over at his place." Well—what'll they know?' He grinned with triumph. 'They won't be none the wiser when we both stay at the Trapp.'

The friends stared as understanding dawned and each expression altered under the pale gaslight. Es had a bright admiring look, George drew in his breath and held it tensely, Polak's slanting cheeks took on a hollow shadow of anxiety.

With a sideways skip, Es cried: 'That's it! Me and Polak can do the same. Then we'd all four of us be there!'

Before he had finished he realized Polak was standing rigid and unresponsive; that the others were watching this reaction. They understood Polak would not approve of such deception. It was a battle between loyalty to the gang and his principles, whose outcome they awaited with strong interest. His cheeks seemed to sink more impassively, his eyes to slant more as he hesitated.

After a while he said: 'Sure thing.'

They walked out of the pool of lamplight content, boots crunching. Round the corner the square tower of St Chad's loomed, the first building of the town. The moon suddenly shone like an arc-lamp turned on and glistened shiftily on the uneven diamond facets of the Gothic windows.

'This is where they ambushed me,' George said. 'They jumped out and held me down and then I escaped and ran by way of the dump. It was there they caught me again and cut off my buttons.'

Through the kissing gate they filed and stood gazing at the transformed scene. A runnel of footsteps led along the snow, spoiling its perfect surface. It wound out of sight among the gravestones towards one corner, and the boys followed this trail, knowing that it would end under the old yew tree that grew against the wall. Here was an established meeting place for Slidden children, summer and winter. Beneath the yew branches was a dry secluded hideout, where eight youngsters could crouch and discuss their affairs in private. For many, many generations back children had met here.

Above, the moon swung behind moving cloud in a blue and amber halo. Shadows of the leafless trees drove sharp and tall across the graveyard, where the elongated shapes of stone crosses, angels and urns stretched black on the whiteness. Nettles and coarse grass that had flourished all summer on the neglected graves now bent under the weight of snow, billowing its surface as though with waves.

Shem led, George next and then Es, who stepped lightly, all at once as nervous as a young colt. Polak glanced behind. They heard a thump.

Es stopped and whispered: 'What's that?'

They looked about, but could see nothing.

'Is it spooks?' Es demanded, stiffening.

'Like as not snow tumbling off bushes,' Polak reassured him.

George said over his shoulder: 'Just the night for spooks.'

Shem chuckled: 'Wouldn't it be great if the graves began to heave up in big white humps, and then all the stiffs pushed out of their coffins? Hey! Look at that one—it's moving!'

All turned in alarm, and Es caught Polak's arm with fierce fingers.

The moon was dimmed by thin cloud that fluttered in shadow form across the snow.

Shem had succeeded in frightening himself as well as his friends. He took two steps back, blundering against George, who exclaimed: 'Get off my corn!'

Polak gave a low laugh and patted Es on the shoulder. 'Forward march!' he said.

Shem stumbled. 'Cor! These brambles act like them trip wires they used for mines in the war.'

'How do you know? You weren't there,' Es said angrily. He was upset by the fright Shem had given him.

'My Dad was there,' Shem replied, ducking under the branches of the yew.

'You go on,' Polak said, shoving Es and turning back.

There under the tree it was dry and windless. The ground was springy with a hundred and sixty seasons of fallen twigs and pin leaves. The boys squatted with their backs against the wall, in which each stone was so deep ingrained with soot that it would not even rub off on their clothes.

'Now what are we going to do?' George asked.

'I dunno why we came.'

'Polak just pushed me,' Es said. He resented that push.

Shem explained: 'We came in automatic like; but there was no need. It's fixed about tomorrow. And you'd all best fetch along any food you can lay hands on. I'll fetch a pack of cards. But I shan't get away till late. I have to help Dad till four.'

Es wriggled and a twig dug into his ear. He whispered: 'It was good the way Polak said he'd do it too. I never thought he'd——'

There was a scuffle and a gasp somewhere.

Shem scrambled out. The moon shone and he could see two figures writhing and tottering. A granite block, topped by an angel with raised arm, seemed to be blessing the combatants, who fell on the soft snow and rolled away. Two boots rose and pressed against an old gravestone, which slowly bent back under the pressure, farther and farther, till at last it fell to the ground with a flump that echoed from the church wall.

Then Polak rose and stood over his enemy, panting. He held a knife that glinted in the moonlight.

'I thought I heard someone sneaking round,' he said. 'Look what he tried on me.'

They all surrounded the vanquished boy.

George exclaimed: 'That's him! That's him what cut off my buttons. That's Red!'

Red rose apprehensively, as well he might.

Shem took the knife from Polak and examined it. 'Nice and sharp.' He glared at the boy. 'So you're the one. Now stick your hands up. Maybe you've more weapons.'

He felt Red slowly, just as he had seen it done on the films. He felt around the waist and fumbled for some time.

'Ay!' cried Red. 'What are you doing?'

There was a movement and Red's trousers crumpled down about his feet. He lowered his arms and pulled them up.

'Come on,' said Shem, pocketing the knife and nudging his friends towards the path. 'I want my tea. We'll leave old trousers to follow.'

They walked off with dignity, out through the other kissing gate and along the lane where the little houses began, row upon row, back to back, front to front of blackened stone, fitted tight against the sloping hill.

Shem's shoulders were shaking, his head ducked.

'Ee, Shem,' Es squeaked. 'What did you do to him?'

Shem tossed back his hair with a jerk and laughed. A lamp lit his gaunt face. He banged his fists up and down on his thighs. 'Ee lad,' he said. 'It was just tit for tat. I cut off his trouser buttons!'

bear the idea of being trapped. 'Aye, but if we dodged behind the tips. We know the tips best.'

'Might be all right if there wasn't snow. Footmarks give you away.'

A distant shout made Es start and stiffen. 'I'm bloody scared,' he said softly. 'They might do anything.'

Polak stood oblivious. 'There must be something in this place—something,' he muttered. His mind sorted through all the metal and wooden objects. The rusty shell of a lorry engine, the scaffold bars, an iron plate bolted down on the shop floor.

'If we could get that up she could be wedged against the window with rods,' he said.

'Get what up?' gasped Es. Then he screeched in angry, hysterical fear. 'Oh, hurry up—do something!'

Polak said: 'Don't agitate, lad.'

He walked into the big room and stared down at the plate; its bolts were rusty, the floor boards appeared immovable.

'Pity. It would have done.'

From outside there came the sound of voices and a thud of snowballs hurled against the great wooden doors. Some-one pushed and the lock rattled.

'What are we going to do?' cried Es, panting.

Polak raised his head. 'Of course—a door! Come on quick! Fetch one of them flat bars—there's a couple laying there.'

He ran along the passage to the old office, swung the door open and gave a violent tug. But the door had been hung during the period when good workmanship was prized, when hinges were strong and wood seasoned. He yelled for Es to hurry, he wrenched at the handle. The sound of metal clanking along the corridor satisfied him, till he saw what Es had brought. In his panic Es had chosen a circular, not a flat, rod.

With a cry of exasperation Polak flung it away and dashed

past to fetch one from the lavatory. Once this was wedged in the crack between the door and the jamb they began to lever. They struggled and gasped as the hinges writhed and the wood creaked and split. Polak let go and stood back to rest his aching arms. His face was blotchy.

'Go and see what they're up to,' he panted. 'Go and clear the bog, so I can get this door in.'

Es went.

Then Polak took a deep breath and dragged on the bar with all his strength. The wood let out a tearing screech, the lower hinge came away and the door swung loose, while Polak tumbled back into the passage, the bar clattering across his chest.

He rose with a sense of achievement, only to realize that the top hinge would now be more difficult to wrench free.

'You should have done the top one first, you nit!' he gasped, with bitter contempt for his own stupidity.

As he considered the problem, he was aware of silence, aware of Es creeping and peeping within, while the others were creeping and peeping without. This morning there was no wind over the snow-hushed land.

A shout: 'There he goes!'

Then concerted cries: 'It's Es! Round this way, lads!'

Polak swung the door out from the top hinge and wrenched. Again the shearing of wood, though the screws held. He pushed with his shoulder, then his arm, straining the whole door outwards, and it twisted above his head and crashed angrily to the ground, free. Clutching it against his hip, Polak dragged the door along the passage, shouting for assistance as he went. Es could be seen backing out of the lavatory with a long pole held before him in both hands, couched like a spear.

Es was yelling so loudly he could not hear his friend. 'Get out! Don't you dare, you scum! Bloody scum!'

He jabbed round the corner, his thin arms jerking, so that

Polak imagined the place must be thick with enemy. But when he pushed Es aside and entered, the lavatory was empty.

A boy's head appeared behind the little window where two pink hands clutched the bars. It was the hands which had sent Es stumbling back. He tried to help with the door, but his fingers would not grip and all the while he jittered, making small noises and exclamations of alarm.

Polak threw the door forward on its edge and it slid among the poles, knocking them away. He then charged in and, inspired with desperate strength, heaved the door up on end. Two startled eyes gaped from the window and a foot lifted seeking a toehold between the bars. The figure wobbled and a voice without exclaimed:

'Get on with it, Al. Your boot's grinding a hole in my back.'

With the door in his arms, Polak stepped forward and, stumbling on a rod, clapped it hard against the window. He stood gasping, all his weight pressed forward, while from without came a cry of indignation, followed by shouts.

'Buck up, Es! Give us the rods!'

The door began to quiver as hands outside pushed.

'Come on you—I can't hold her!'

Es obeyed. Rods were wedged diagonally from the top of the door to the wall, where they jammed at the angle with the floor. Five of them fixed it immovably. After a while the Bullman boys gave up their futile shoving and banging and insults.

Then Es led the way up to the store-room, where they could keep watch.

Polak said: 'That was a near one.' He spun round on one leg like a top, tumbled and sat on the dirty floor chuckling triumphantly. 'You know what, Esmond Cattermole? We're besieged.'

6

It was not much fun being besieged. There was nothing to do, except keep the fire going. There was no food. The Bullman gang lurked, taking turns to go off for dinner or other occupations, while hour after hour passed. During the afternoon Polak and Es again practised their acrobatics, but their limbs were stiff with cold and their bodies soon grew tired. Es found a dirty sugar lump in his pocket, which he was saving for a horse, and this they halved and ate. Later they poured boiling water on the old tea leaves in the teapot and drank the pallid hot water.

Es said: 'This is like China tea, what posh folk drink. Cat piss I call it.'

'Cat piss is stronger,' Polak replied.

'Hey—where's our Fleabag? He can't climb in at the toilet window now.'

'He's not one to be kept out—he's like me,' Polak replied. 'We might as well stock up with fuel. Wood burns that quick.'

So they went back to the store-room. Outside the sky was a hard grey and slow snowflakes fell far apart and solitary. The white moor, the hillocks and the slag heaps were drab in the dull light, not sparkling as they had been under the morning sun. Faintly St Chad's rang out: bong, bong.

'Only two,' wailed Es. 'What are we going to do? I dursn't go home tonight after I told them I was staying out with you. There's nothing to eat, nothing to sleep on, nothing to do. Let's run for it.'

'If Shem hadn't cut off Red's buttons it might be worth the risk. But—look there——'

Es stood on tiptoe and peered out of the window. A boy was creeping along against the mill wall and in his hand was a rough fencing stake with a pointed end. He held it like a spear.

'How about if we dropped an oil can on his head?'

'Waste of a good can,' Polak replied.

The boy passed out of sight and the landscape was still.

'I wish some of our lads would come,' Es wailed.

A flapping, whinnying sound startled them and a pigeon settled in an empty window frame, rocking. It peeped into the room and, with a huge flurry of wings, landed on the dusty floor. The back was silver grey, a white collar round the neck and red feet; the pinky mauve breast feathers fluffed out as the bird put its head on one side and stared around jerkily, then hunched its shoulders and stepped forward. It pecked something in the dust, decided it tasted bad and, with a twitch of the head, flung it aside.

The boys had remained still, but now Es dashed forward to make a grab. With a flash of wings the pigeon flew to the farthest window, rocking again as it balanced on the iron frame, and then disappeared into the grey.

'You devil!' cried Es.

'He had a bad look in his eye,'

'If I could have caught him, we could have cooked him.'

There was a silence as they imagined roast pigeon. Then Polak clapped his hands and rubbed his fingers together. 'Come on, we have to make a store of wood for the night. It'll be dark soon. You fill the kettle with snow first.'

In the workshop Polak struggled to lever up a floor board.

37

He inserted the flat iron bar in a splintered crack and heaved and pressed alternately, but the bar kept jumping out. Es hopped from one leg to the other like a bobbin, blue and useless, shaking his hands to warm them.

'Stop that jigging and give us a hand!' Polak exclaimed. 'Hold here, while I bash.'

He banged the bar with another rod and, once firmly wedged, they both put their weight on the end. The board creaked, resisted, shifted, then moved. Slowly it rose till, suddenly, with a shriek, the nails tore out of the joists, and the boys floundered back.

'That's a stupid thick plank,' Es said.

'Just think of the weight it had to support. Great carding machines and such. You'd best start sawing, while I try the next one. They'll come easier now.'

At the third ten-foot plank the iron bar snapped in two. Polak said nothing, as was his habit in moments of crisis, but stood and stared at his fiery red palms. He would not permit Es to stop sawing, though his thin arms ached and he worked slower and slower. Polak knew they must keep moving to resist the cold and boredom that sapped their strength.

Every so often he would walk to the window to see whether the Bullman gang was still about. No human movement was visible. The sky grew darker, snow fell gently.

Echoing through the empty building the boards were bumped upstairs and the fire revived. Half way on the second journey Es stopped.

'What's that? Listen!'

A tapping could be heard, sharp, regular, insistent.

They ran down eagerly, but on coming to the lavatory stopped, fearful. The tapping on the wedged door came from outside.

Polak cried: 'Who's that?'

'Let me in!' George's hoarse croak called back.

'Is that you, George?' Es asked anxiously.

'Of course it is! Let me in, I'm stone cold!'

'We'll haul you up,' Polak called. 'We can't shift this lot. Hey—George—did you see any of them?'

'Come on, come on! Let down that rope!'

Once the doors were open, Polak and Es stared from the loading bay onto the heads of three figures stamping their feet and flapping their arms. Two backs were loaded.

Es saw the flopping hair and cried in horror: 'They're girls! We don't want girls!'

But a smiling bearded face turned up to him.

It was hard work pulling George in first. Once the handle caught on Polak's blister and spun through his palms, so that George would have tumbled to the ground, had not Es already belayed the slack as he had been taught.

'We need a proper winch,' gasped Polak. 'Loop her back, lad.'

So George, climbing the last few yards on his own, came over the sill and stamped the snow off his boots.

'Who are they?'

'A bloke and a bird I picked up.'

'Hang on down there. Send up the gear first.'

'Mind my guitar,' a girl's clear voice called.

Once safely arrived, the boys saw that the couple were old, around twenty, and students by their trailing striped scarves. The girl's hair fell down her back in thick dark waves. Her face was pale and handsome, with great warm brown eyes that watched. She wore a pale leather coat from which white fur pressed out all round the edges, and jeans and black boots.

The young man wore steel-rimmed glasses that enlarged his weak eyes. Black hair curled over his collar behind, his beard curled over in front. He stooped and appeared abashed by Es's curious stare, unlike the girl who grinned back. Yet he did not lack confidence when he spoke with a neat middle-class accent.

'This is a fine place you have here.'

'Come in to the fire and make yourselves at home,' George said. 'How about tea, Polak lad?' He was ashamed at the lack of amenities in the Trapp.

'Did you meet up with the Bullman gang?' Es demanded.

'Nay, we didn't see anyone.'

Es exploded indignantly: 'We've been hemmed in since morning and nothing to eat! There was ten of them after us. We're right starved, Polak and me.'

The girl crouched in the firelight and put out her hand to the cat.

'What a marvellous big puss.'

Fleabag laid back his ears and hissed.

Polak warned her: 'Best take care. He's wild. And he's riddled with fleas.'

She drew in her hand and put it to the fire, smiling. 'A sensitive cat.'

Polak said: 'Then, if you weren't bothered, they must have given up and gone home. I'd best go back to town and help Shem bring out summat to eat and bedding.' He kept glancing at the strangers, who made him feel awkward. He did not like them.

'I'll come too,' Es cried.

Polak shook his head. He knew that in case of trouble Es would not be quick enough. Es whined in vain.

'You have to entertain guests with bright prattle,' George snubbed him.

'Come and see me down,' Polak said to his friends.

They left the couple by the fire.

'You're that mean,' Es said, while Polak buttoned his jacket.

'Watch out!' Polak called as he slid away.

It felt dangerous to be in the open once more. Polak stood looking for signs of the enemy. He listened. Everything was still, except for the distant giant pair of iron wheels at the pit head, half of which could be seen behind a tip, slowly turning in opposite directions. The sheds and the scaffold were hidden. Then coal trucks began to clank softly in the afternoon stillness. Polak loved this sound : all his life he had lived within earshot of the musical jingle and clang of trucks. It reminded him that he would be starting work in the mine as soon as he was free of school. He wondered about the 'O' levels he was not taking.

'If we had more staff you could have been pushed through,' old Mac had said to him. 'But you're not the studious type that can work on your own, are you?'

He walked swiftly beside the mill wall, studying footprints partly obliterated by snow. At the same time he was considering how to pay for food. He could probably work off the debt by serving in Scanlon's store all Saturday next weekend, but it was possible they would not need extra hands. His feet hurt with cold, the snow crunched, the sky was as hard and flat as an iron plate. He was on his own, free and happy.

A crow flew up from behind the chimney stack. Polak paused, alert. There sounded a faint breathy whistle. Polak turned and fled.

Behind came a drawn-out yell: 'Come—on! We've got him!'

More shouts and the soft thud of many feet.

'Round the back!'

'Head him off!'

Polak ran faster than he had ever run, even in school races. The long stone wall was beside him. He felt he was gaining, but knew that he must gain a great deal to allow time to climb back. And would Es have heeded his last words, 'Watch out!' He ran as he had been taught, elbows in, chin forward, knees up, relaxed, determined. The cold air and the cries behind spurred him on. He was round the corner and saw to his dismay that the hauled-up rope was just out of reach.

He yelled with a last strangled breath: 'Es! Hoy! Es!' and fell against the wall.

The muffled thump of boots grew louder.

Polak shifted his back along until it was in the centre of the great doors and, leaning there exhausted, prepared to fight. In between gasps for breath he heard voices from the other side of the mill, and knew that they would close in from both sides.

There was a rattle. The rope came hurtling down.

Polak sprang just as the enemy rounded the corner. His fingers clutched, his feet crossed and drew in on the thick hemp like pincers. Up he went in rhythmic jerks, arms stretching above, hauling, straightening and flexing like a concertina. Way below came the shouts of thwarted violence. He passed the top of the doors and knew he was out of reach. Here, for a moment, he rested. Then at once the rope began to shake and twist, so that his boots lost their grip and he slipped back to arms' length. There was a yell from those below. His hands held while he regained a foothold and heaved his body up. For the first time he looked over his arm at the upturned faces, open gazing eyes, open howling mouths, hands raised and fingers spread, ready to tear him to pieces the moment he fell among the pack.

'George gave us the slip—you're not going to!' someone bawled.

He was unnerved.

Another voice cried: 'We'll cut off every button on your body!'

The rope gave a violent twitch.

Es's high voice called above him: 'Come on, Polak! You'll do it! We're here!'

So he dragged himself up another arm's length.

Now the rope stopped wriggling and the Bullman gang argued among themselves.

'You go, Norman. You're best at climbing. Catch him by the ankle. He'll soon tumble.'

But Norman did not like the appearance of the metal hob-nails shining on the soles of Polak's boots.

'Try it yourself!' he retorted angrily.

Polak was breathing heavily, his arms were weakening, his energy waning, when something hit him on the back, wang! Cold splashed his cheek. He saw a snowball burst against the mill wall. The thuds became louder and he knew they were pressing the snow till it was tight-packed like ice— cannon-balling it was called. The bombardment continued till he was hit on the head so hard his mind dazed. He swayed out drunkenly, and again the pack yelled.

But the husky whisper of George was above: 'Three more pulls and you're there, lad!'

'Stick to it! We're here!' piped Es.

Polak's mind was stupid with the pain in his head; his weary arms seemed almost dragged from their sockets. He moved automatically. With another spring from the knees he saw the wooden ledge of the platform and the cracked toe-caps on George's old boots, their soles parted from the uppers and the stitches broken. Fingers tugged at the collar of his jacket.

Now the gang was trying to swing the rope away from the loading bay, while George grasped the upper end and tried to drag it in.

Polak made another effort, caught the ledge, lost his hold and was almost torn off the rope by Es.

'Look out!' he gasped, and flung himself over the sill, to be caught and pulled in by his friends.

George went onto the bay again and gave the rope a sudden tug that tore it from the hands below. Then he pulled it out of reach, while they howled and pelted. He stepped back and clanged the doors to.

Es knelt beside Polak, his face stiff and white with anxiety.

43

He gave a quick glance at George, who stepped beside the collapsed body.

'Do you think he's all right?'

'I dunno. He don't look it.'

Polak shifted his head, for his mouth was sucking dust. He opened his eyes to see once again two scarred leather domes.

'Your boots always give me hope, George,' he whispered.

7

An hour later George and Es were still unable to compose themselves. Es sat on the packing case and, pressing his hollow stomach with his hands, rocked back and forth to allay the pangs of hunger. He was not accustomed to hunger like George, or able to bear it like Polak.

George walked round and round staring at the floor, with his whiskery eyebrows twitching up and down. He sometimes muttered aloud, for he was drafting an article for the local newspaper about the Trapp. It was highly melodramatic.

The couple had undone their bedding rolls and settled on the far side of the fire, she curled on her side, he lying with his head against her hip. Both were apparently asleep.

The young man had given an explanation when they first lay down. 'We were at a party all last night and got a lift out of London around six o'clock. We'll take a nap if you don't mind. It's good to come indoors on a day like this. Cold on the road.'

Polak frowned, Es opened his mouth, while George pretended disinterest. But the room remained heavy with the strangers' silent, disturbing presence.

Only Polak was still stimulated by the siege. He had cut and stacked more wood, he went about the mill and ascertained that the gang had not left, but were sheltering in the chimney stack and must have missed George and the southerners through inattention. He stuffed the kettle with snow and brought it to the boil, though there was no tea. His face was serious yet content as he considered their problems.

'Aren't you bothered?' Es asked in a nervous whine.

Polak stood before the fire, warming the backs of his legs. He spoke in his calm, rough voice, newly broken.

'In the war my Dad was blown up on his trawler—a torpedo one night. They was all drowned, all but him and his mate. So they found themselves on one of these rafts, sloshing up and down in the dark, hour after hour. It was like now—cold—January—only they were somewhere up near the north part of Norway—the Arctic. You imagine that black and that cold and the waves as high as this mill, and that raft and two men. There they sat till dawn comes up, and then they saw the cliffs, great black cliffs in front of them, coming near. So they stood up to be ready to jump, and the spray shoots off the rocks. So after a bit my Dad says, he says: "Get ready, Joe." But Joe doesn't answer. So my Dad turns and lays his hand on Joe's shoulder, friendly like, and Joe falls flat on his face into the sea, stiff as a poker. He'd iced up.'

Es's mouth opened with horror.

George remarked: 'I do believe you like problems, Polak. You revel in them.' He made a disgusted face.

'That's all life is. Best attack them, than let them attack you. That's what I say. It's problems are the interesting part, if you look at it rightly.' He saw that the girl's eyes were staring at him fixedly.

'Rightly!' George exclaimed with scorn. 'And do you know what rightly is, lad?'

Polak was silent. Then spoke slowly. 'Aye, I know what rightly is for me—well—sometimes any rate.' He grew more doubtful as he thought about it.

'So what! It's all in the mind!' George mocked. 'But Es's

mind and your mind and my mind are different. You can fetch Es up short with a spider. And me—I don't like having my arm twisted. It's not an interesting sensation to me. But as for you—you're our wonder boy, you lucky lad!'

Polak stared at the steaming kettle, scared by the bitterness in George's voice. Es jerked his hand back and forth from the wrist like a shuttle, shocked to hear his idol castigated. Flames spurted and dwindled along splinters of wood.

George turned sharply to face the strangers.

'Hey, you, where do you come from?' he asked.

The young man opened his eyes and picked up his spectacles.

'London.'

'You on the road?'

'Sort of.'

The girl broke in impatiently: 'What do you mean, sort of, Christopher? Yes, we're on the road till next term.'

Es exclaimed with indignation: 'Our term's been started these two weeks.'

'We're at college, Es. At least I am. Longer holidays, you know.' She smiled from one to another.

Polak stared stolidly. He had never met a girl, or a boy for that matter, from college.

'Do you go to the tec?' George asked.

'No, Lucy's in medical school. I'm starting as a reporter on the *Muswell Hill Star* in a fortnight.'

'Will you be a real doctor?' Es demanded of the girl.

Lucy opened her eyes wide, a friendly eagerness in her face, her voice a little mocking.

'Why not?'

The superior education of their guests awed the boys, except George who was determined not to be awed.

He said: 'I'll work on a paper too when I leave school. But I'm not going in at the top like you. *Murthwaite Post*. I'll be lucky if I'm licking stamps.'

47

'That's an old-fashioned idea of newspaper life,' the girl said.

'Aye, that's what we are up here—old-fashioned.'

'Don't be put off if you aren't lucky,' Chistopher advised, kindly pompous, twiddling his beard.

There was silence. The northerners and the southerners were not pleased with each other.

Es exclaimed angrily: 'It's just bloody boring being cooped up here!'

Polak fetched the saw that leant against the wall and handed it to Es.

'So you're bored. Right. You go and cut next load. You'll find a plank ripped up in the shop.'

For a moment it seemed as though Es would rebel. He was near to tears. He hesitated, then snatched the saw and stamped out.

'And shut the door after you!' yelled Polak.

He lifted the kettle off the fire, remarking: 'He's hungry, that's his trouble.'

'Hey, Lucy,' said Chistopher. 'We've still got some chocolate and cheese. The poor kid.'

George raised his eyebrows as a signal to Polak.

''Twas a pity I couldn't get through,' Polak apologized generally. 'But I didn't fancy being roughed up by that lot, not after what Shem did to Red.'

George said: 'Have you noticed, when folk say they're bored they don't mean that one bit. They mean angry, only they won't own up.'

He rose, opened the desk lid and took out the black book.

'I'll write an account,' he said.

Polak stared in his simplicity.

'Nay, an account of the Trapp. All what we've done. There's nowt else to do.'

Polak gazed at the book coldly.

'You go ahead.'

George fished out the ink bottle and a rusty pen.

'Here,' Lucy said, 'I've a ball pen.'

She searched her pockets and rucksack, but could find none. Christopher also searched in vain.

'Think of coming away and nothing to write with—how extraordinary, extraordinary!' she exclaimed.

Polak shook his head at this affectation. His slanting cheek-bones and grey eyes took on an obstinate dead look. Then he smiled to see George's disconsolate face and the hopeless way in which he picked at the rust on the old nib. George was very proud of his copperplate handwriting, which so infuriated the teachers at school. Polak lifted the kettle and dribbled hot water into the ink bottle. Then he carefully scraped rust from the nib with his thumb nail and made the metal pliable.

When Es returned, puffing pink-cheeked and triumphant, a bundle of banisters under each arm, the room was quiet. George was filling a third page with his elegant loops and squirls, Christopher was reading a paperback, Lucy lay asleep, while Polak sat and stared at her.

'Banisters came down a treat,' Es said.

'You're burning the banisters!' Christopher exclaimed, shocked.

'Must keep warm,' Polak retorted.

'We've a bit of food, if you'd like it, Es. Hey, wake up, Lucy. Where's that chocolate and stuff?'

The sight of brown chocolate, yellow cheese and three green apples was almost more than the boys could bear. Es broke into one of his delighted jigs, George goggled. But Polak controlled unseemly interest, though his mouth filled with saliva.

'Read us what you wrote, George,' he said. 'It'll pass the time till I can get through and fetch more grub.'

George suffered no false modesty about his compositions, for in school he was often asked to read them out. But his mouth was in imagination full of chocolate and cheese and apple.

'Hold on a minute,' he said.

Es clattered the banisters into the corner, the food was shared and eaten. Then George turned his book to catch the firelight, for the brightness in the sky was fading.

'It's not much,' he said, and began to read in a solemn husky voice:

'This is a kind of log book, like if we never escape from the Trapp alive. Then someone will find it and be able to tell what happened to some good friends. Because we've a problem, and that is no one knows where we are. Leastways only the Bullman gang and they won't split. It's they who will have killed us.

'The Trapp is surrounded by the Bullman Lane gang, but they can't get in. It is two to one, so we dursn't try anything like climbing out or bashing them up. Shem would laugh if he knew. He laughs at everything, does Shem. Polak tried to sneak by and fetch our lads from town, and the dinner, but he was near enough caught and had to run for it. He climbed back and they cannon-balled him. They haven't anyone can climb like our Polak. They tried to shake him loose, but he held on like a monkey. We hauled him in half dead just in time.

'There's not a scrap to eat in the place, only luckily I brought along two southerners, or we'd be right starved. Es just carried in a faggot of banisters to keep us warm through the night. Wood burns that fast, and the moor outside lousy with coal. It sickens you to think on it. The old stairway won't look the same now. It's rare cold.'

There was silence from the impressed strangers.

'Our George is a dab hand at this writing lark,' Polak said, making what he considered a joke. But no one smiled.

'It's good, very good,' Christopher said, nodding judicially.

'You sound like a beastly school master,' Lucy said. 'Still, I think it's fine too. Now you write something, Polak.'

Polak shook his head.

'Hand over. I'll write a poem,' Es volunteered. 'But it won't be much good.'

'We all know that,' George said.

Es was not put off. He took the book, the pen and ink and sat on his packing case, chewing his little finger nail, while the others talked a little more easily now.

Lucy asked: 'How long do your sieges usually last?'

George said: 'This is how it would be in the olden days besieged in a castle. Cooped up month after month, year in year out. And look how it is with us. Fed up after a few hours. Think if this was a week.'

They considered living in the Trapp like this for a week.

'Aye,' Polak said. 'But if it were the olden days I'd be making cannon-balls and sharpening swords, and that stuff. I wouldn't half mind working in an armoury.'

Christopher said: 'But in the end there'd come a time when your iron was all used up. You'd be stuck with nothing to do, just as we are now.'

Polak retorted: 'There's always things need doing round the place, like any home. I mean, we need a new ballcock in our toilet, and Tyotyr Nina wants a shelf in her room. Just think what a castle needs. Walls repaired, horses fed, wood chopped——'

Es looked up and interrupted: 'They didn't have ballcocks, they just pissed out of arrow slits.'

George said lugubriously: 'You wouldn't want to do that, Es, if the enemy was a good shot.'

They laughed.

'Ah!' cried Polak, jumping up and feeling in his pocket. 'You know what I got for you, George? They're beauties!

Tyotyr Nina presents them to Mr George with compliments!'

He took out a neat little package of blue velvet and opened it carefully on the floor before the fire. Inside were a black cotton reel and eight buttons, diamond-shaped black-and-gold metal buttons. A needle was threaded through the velvet.

Lucy raised herself to look.

Es exclaimed: 'Ee, they're lovely! You aren't half lucky, George.'

At this George inspected the buttons more closely.

'A bit flash,' he said dubiously, and backed away.

'I'll have them!' Es cried. 'I'll stick them on my jacket.'

George spoke hastily: 'I didn't say no. I only said a bit outlandish.'

'That's just what they are. They come from my country,' Polak said, offended. 'If they aren't welcome——'

But before he could gather them up, George had taken one, drawn his dangling waistcoat together, and gazed down at the effect on the black and white pin stripe.

'What do you think?' he asked doubtfully, looking round to Lucy.

Polak shrugged his shoulders and turned away. But Es, anxious to placate both friends, put his arm round Polak's shoulder, pulled him, back, set his curly head on one side and said in his most cooing tone: 'Bloody perfect! You look, Polak, it's bloody perfect!'

Lucy and Christopher laughed.

'Take her off,' Polak said, picking up the needle and thread.

'Are you going to sew them?'

'You're not going to, that's for sure,' Polak replied.

George tugged off his old coat and declaimed with a vacant face: 'Our Polak sews a pretty seam.'

'You could do with embroidery lessons yourself,' Polak

said, pointing to the tattered lining that dropped away from the arm holes. He gave Lucy an antagonistic stare, as though daring her to offer to sew for him. However, she remained silent.

The room was quiet again, Polak stitched and Es bent, nail biting, over his poem. The couple whispered together. George daydreamed, his cheek near the fire bright red. He spoke after a long silence, as Polak bit off the thread for the fifth button.

'I think I'm clever. But I'm not sure I'm clever enough. I keep asking myself, "Will you do it? Have you the guts, lad?"'

'Do what?' Christopher asked.

'It's not hard work—that doesn't worry me. But it's the way to get in with the right folk. Thought I might ask a reporter from the *Murthwaite Post* to come out here and take a look. Then I could write my version and he could use it.'

The brown varnish on a banister bubbled in big blisters and melted softly, while the rising and falling flame seeped along the wood.

'You see, you've got to start by licking stamps—and boots. But if I was in with the boys I'd be on my way.'

George sighed, rubbed his red cheek with one hand and poked at a fiery banister with the other. Wind blew in gusts round the mill and whined along the passages. Es kept dipping the pen in the pale ink and scratching out words.

Polak held up the finished waistcoat. 'You'd best be a circus clown, George. Put her on while I cobble up that lining.'

8

Christopher stood twiddling his beard before the fire.

'My sister thinks your Bullman boys wouldn't do anything to her if she went to buy the food.'

'Your sister?' demanded Polak. 'I thought you were——'

'Yes, my brother,' Lucy said and jumped up. 'I feel fine now. I'll go. They wouldn't dare——'

'I wouldn't be too sure,' George said. 'Norman and Al are big lads. They're older than us.'

Polak added: 'I wouldn't trust Red neither. We took a flick knife off him last night.'

Christopher's confidence was shaken. 'Oh, I see.' He bit his lips, the upper then the lower, with a quick shifting of his teeth. 'We don't want headlines: "Girl Cut Up on Moor". We don't want that.'

'Don't be silly! Of course they wouldn't!' Lucy snapped. But there was a nervous change in her voice. 'Come on, Es. Let's take a look at the enemy.'

'You coming?' Es asked, with an anxious glance at Polak.

So the three of them went down the stone stair, where the stumps of banisters sprouted like the remains of badly felled trees. And across the hall below lay the curving mahogany rail fallen from above.

'I did that,' Es boasted.

A wail rang out, a soaring screech, sinking and soaring three times, grating on their nerves like a file. Then all was quiet in the greyness.

'What's that?' Lucy demanded huskily.

'That's the same as last night,' Polak whispered.

'I'm not coming,' Es gasped.

He ran back up the stairs and into the front room, slamming the door.

'We'd better see what's up,' Lucy said with an effort.

They descended slowly, the terrible cry curling and scraping through their memories.

Polak did not speak, but systematically inspected each room and out of each window, treading softly, his heart athump. Every time they came back to the big hall they stood listening, as though having once heard the screech from this position it would recur there. Indeed it was from here that they heard another unexpected sound. A bumping from somewhere beyond the passage that led to the back door. Across from this door, securely shut with bolts and a great mortice lock, stood the tumbled chimney stack and sheds in which the Bullman gang sheltered.

Lucy and Polak tiptoed to the door and listened to the bumps and scraping.

Then came boys' voices.

'Don't be daft.'

'Who's daft? Bring it over.'

'Look out. It'll never burn.'

'We'll smoke them out.'

'Course it will. Once you set that door alight they've had it.'

'Give them a call, Fordyce.'

'I can't.'

'Course you can. I bet Es Cattermole fainted when he heard you.'

'I done it twice. My voice won't.'

'Go on, or I'll give you something to make you.'

'I can't.'

'Go on, you.'

Although they were prepared, Lucy and Polak both jumped as the screech broke from the other side of the door. A nightmare scream, now forced and hoarse.

A moment later there were footsteps leaping downstairs two at a time and Christopher rushed into the dim passage. He stopped beside his sister and sniffed the smell of burning wood. A drift of smoke seeped through the keyhole and under the lintel.

'What on earth——'

The gang outside had heard the bounding footsteps.

'We know you're there, Polak!'

'We've got you now!'

'The door's on fire!'

'Hey, George, we're going to skin you alive and frizzle your waistcoat!'

A gust of wind buffeted against the building and the stout door shuddered. Another flurry of air rushed past whining. The passage was misted with smoke.

'Barbarians!' Christopher muttered.

They retreated to the hall and saw Es and George at the top of the stairs, too nervous to come down and too nervous to stay alone.

'What's up?' George called.

'They're trying to set the place on fire.'

'Snow's coming down like a blanket. You can't see an inch,' Es said.

'That'll settle their bonfire—I hope. Barbarians!' Christopher repeated.

Indeed it seemed unlikely that the Bullman gang would stay abroad in the storm that had suddenly swept over the moor.

'That's settled their bonfire,' Es echoed triumphantly as he poked up the blaze in the front room.

'Come along, Es,' Christopher urged. 'Read us your poem now. We will have to make do with intellectual food.'

'Go on,' George added. 'Shem isn't here to take the mickey out of you. Have a go!'

Es's voice quavered with nervousness. The words, written in watery ink and scratched out and blotched, came jerkily in a stiff falsetto.

'My belys empty it mones its noring
sitting here is blody boreing
We carnt get out
bullman lads are a bout
no one wuld here if you gav a shout
the trapp is a long way of from town.
Fish and chips give me fish and chips
a chip on my lip
and a bit of fish
in news papper with out a dish
thats the best thing i wish
for us pore begers.'

Es explained: 'You see, it won't do it at the end—it just won't.'

George felt critical. 'You want to work out the rhythm you want. You want to——' He stopped speaking and edged his boot away from Fleabag, who had stretched his stomach to the warmth. George pushed up his trouser leg and began to scratch his white leg ferociously. 'Fleas! That cat ought to be fumigated.'

Es yawned loudly, squeezed his eyes shut and kept them shut. 'It won't half be cold tonight.'

'If I could of broken through I could of fetched back blankets and stuff.'

'What?'

'I just said—nothing.'

Silence. Each sat absorbed in his own dream. George

hunched, Polak relaxed, Es rocking back and forth. Christopher had pushed up his glasses and rubbed his face abstractedly, Lucy appeared to doze once more.

'Aye—tell us a Tyotyr story, Polak!' Es exclaimed suddenly, his face at once eager and shining.

To everyone's surprise Polak began immediately, speaking somewhat mechanically at first, but soon warming to the tale.

'Once upon a time there was an old witch. She was that old—hundreds of years—no one could remember when she—when she hadn't lived by the side of the river in her little hut. It was a great wide slow river, like we have back home.'

When Polak spoke of Poland as his home George always raised his tufty black eyebrows and cleared his throat. He did so now.

'You shut up, George,' Polak said.

'She had weeny needle eyes and a great big quick-smelling nose. And when fishermen sailed by she would sing out——' Polak paused, translating first in his mind.

'"Fisherman, fisherman, don't you dare pass me by,
   I must have fish for my dinner today."

'Fishermen were scared not to stop and give her their best—or she would put the evil eye on them. Then they wouldn't catch not a sprat, and the kids would go hungry and crying. Still, it was hard when fish were scarce to give up your best to that old hag.'

'Why didn't they chop her head off?' Es demanded.

'Kill a witch!' Polak exclaimed. 'Don't you know the way it is? They come more and more. Chop off one hand and there's two grow on the stump; chop off a head and there's four eyes staring back at you! The only way I know is strong poison, like for rats, but they didn't have strychnine round them parts.

'Well, anyway, there was this young lad lived with his

sister—she was that beautiful, but simple like. And he made up his mind to trick the old witch, for he was in the middle of building a boat and he needed more wood. They lived alone because when they were kids that witch had put a curse on his Mum and Dad, and that killed them off quick sharp. So one night, when it was pitch dark, young Ivan lets his boat drift down river, past her hut, and then he puts out his net and sets a lantern in the stern. Then he has good luck. Fishes come to look at light, just like moths, and before daybreak he rowed back to the village, softly as he knew how, with the boat low in the water. When he knocked five times, his sister unbolted the door and let him in, like he always told her. Next day they took the load of fish and sold them in the market, and Ivan bought his wood. So that was a bit of all right.

'But the old witch was no fool. She wondered why Ivan never went by, day after day, and she watched and waited. But when she got no clue she ups and asks the fishermen. They just shook their wooden heads, they knew nothing; but only one man. He was a fellow had been after the sister to marry him, for she may have been simple, but she had lovely gold hair and a good temper. She told him straight she'd rather stay on with her brother, so he was right vexed. Then he went to Ivan and offers him a cow; but Ivan says: "Nay, she shall do as she wishes."

'So this fellow looks wise and says to the witch: "Ee," he says, "can't you guess? My guess is he goes out by nights."

'Then she was real vexed and set on punishing the lad.'

Polak rubbed his hand across his mouth and laid another banister on the fire. The room was dark now.

'Aye, she was that vexed her hair stood like bristles on a brush and she made bad faces.'

A sound like drumming came from the distance. It had gradually sunk into their consciousness. Es jumped up, his face drained of colour, George leant forward, his eyes rolled to the top of their sockets. Polak raised one hand.

'Best see what's up.'

George gave a forced laugh.

Polak withdrew a flaming banister from the fire and led the way out and downstairs. Christopher followed.

'They're outside toilet,' George said.

'Nay—aye—you're right.'

Es was stumbling about behind. Polak held the torch high to light the stairs, but the draught made the flame jerk back and forth, its strength diminished. Then suddenly there was only a red glow.

'Keep your hand on the wall now banisters are gone,' Polak ordered.

The drumming, which had stopped momentarily, recommenced, then stopped as a voice called: 'Hey—you there?'

They paused at the bottom of the stairway.

'Because if you aren't I'm off.'

Es said: 'It's a trick. Look out.'

Polak roared: 'Is that you, Shem?'

'You dumb cluck—now they know!' George exclaimed.

They edged forward, irritated with each other, yet not daring to show their full anger.

'Don't push, lad,' Polak said.

It was surprisingly difficult to find the way in the dark. The distance from one place to another was always farther than expected; the lavatory door, swinging open under the weight of Polak's hand, felt like the wall giving way. He called again.

Shem's voice replied impatiently: 'Hurry up! I've been banging for hours.'

'You'll have to come up by rope. We can't shift this lot in the dark.'

Es chipped in: 'Are the Bullman lads with you?'

'Don't be daft,' George muttered. 'He dursn't say if they are.'

'Go round the front,' Polak cried. 'We'll pull you up.' He whispered to his friends: 'Then we'll see who's there.'

So they fumbled back upstairs and through the storeroom, where light from the reflecting snow made it possible to see greyly.

Shem stood below, alone.

When he had been hauled in, he reported that the Bullman gang had returned to town. He had seen them by the church, eight of them, and had hidden behind a gravestone till they passed.

As usual the brother and sister sat side by side watching. All at once Shem strode over, tossed back his lock of hair, and demanded:

'What are you looking at then?'

Christopher glanced aside, but Lucy raised her head and stared in Shem's face.

'I'm sorry,' she said evenly. 'We don't mean to be rude. Only it's like coming to a foreign country, you know.'

'Can't say I do,' Shem retorted.

Polak interrupted, suggesting that he and George should go to buy the necessary stores, if Shem did not fancy another walk in the cold.

'Why can't I ever come?' Es whined.

'Youngsters do what they're told,' Polak said, leading the way out of the room.

George was detained by the girl at the door. She laid a hand on his sleeve and spoke in a slow soft voice.

'Just a minute. Would you buy tobacco for fags, and papers? The rest will do for food. You see, we expected to pay for a bed tonight at the hostel. Get what you think best.' She pushed some money into George's knobbly fingers. 'And thanks ever so.'

George hunched his shoulders, embarrassed.

Polak's voice called from the loading bay: 'Hurry on, George. Rope's down.'

9

Slidden was busy with Saturday night coming and going when George and Polak walked up the High Street. There was a small queue for the cinema. At the front stood Red, his blazing hair greased smooth, his cheeks shiny from the wash. Against him leant a girl like a doll, round head, shingled hair and black eyelashes, dressed in a short skirt with well stuffed pink legs coming out.

Seeing this pair, Polak pulled George and they turned down a side road, satisfied to know that Red was out of the way for the night. Past the Old White Bear Wrestling Club, built of richly blackened brick, with its slogan, 'Be Strong and Defend Yourself', past the Methodist Hall, built in coldly blackened stone, with a cry in fluorescent tangerine: 'Lay up for yourselves Treasures in Heaven'.

George paused and denounced sonorously: 'Lay up for yourselves treasures in Heaven—there's no hope down here, mates.' Then he burst into his mocking falsetto laugh.

Polak marched on. His Catholic upbringing could not stomach such levity, even though it concerned a rival church. Yet in his own way he was critical of Catholic activities and had once confided to George he couldn't stomach the local priest.

The back street grocery stores were still open; but they

avoided those frequented by locals, in case gossip should get back to the family. George stopped under a lamp that lit the brown sludge of snow and pulled the coins from his pocket. To his disappointment it only came to eighty pence.

'Where's that come from?' Polak demanded sharply, hand in his own trouser pocket, feeling for the money saved for this occasion.

George tossed his head. 'That girl gave it me. She wants tobacco for fags, and food with the rest.'

Polak frowned. He did not approve that a stranger, a girl, should provide them with money. 'You shouldn't have took it.'

'You didn't want her coming along, did you?'

They considered how her exotic appearance in Slidden would have embarrassed them. Polak said no more.

They shopped in a dingy, lonely store.

Beans

Two sliced loaves

Half of marg

A dozen cracks

Six gob stoppers

Two pounds of broken biscuits

One candle

The oil stove stank, wind rattled a door at the back of the shop and a grey-faced woman with heavy hips dragged herself about. Breath wheezed as it came from her chest, as though she needed oiling. She found a cardboard box for the food, which delighted Polak, who longed to furnish the Trapp with conveniences.

'Any more boxes?' he asked.

'Not for you, luv,' she replied and hissed the breath between her teeth. 'Oh, my tubes—they're seized up!' She laid her hand on her chest and looked from one boy to the other to hold their attention. 'This cold creeps up your skirt at the back and down your neck in front. Tedious weather.'

'An ounce of tobacco for fags,' George interrupted.

'Aye, it catches you. The air can't get out once it's gone in. How are you for tea? Aye—and sugar?'

'We can't pay for sugar—only tea.'

The woman put back the packet she had just lifted from the shelf and turned.

'Right—is that the lot?'

'I'll pay for the sugar next week.'

'Is that the lot?'

'How much is sugar?' Polak insisted obstinately.

'Where do you come from?'

'Murthwaite Terrace.'

'Do you know Mary Gorman?'

'Aye—she's opposite at number forty.'

'Don't forget then.' She lifted down the sugar.

The next problem was bedding. After much hesitation Polak decided to raid his own home. He could tell his mother that Es had not enough blankets to go round.

'And that's true,' George said with a grin.

They climbed to the terrace where Polak lived by steps that ran straight up the hillside between high stone walls. The way was so narrow Polak had to carry the cardboard box on top of his head.

'You look like a bloody native,' George gasped as he struggled to keep up.

Half way there was a landing where people paused to rest. Below lay tiers of roof tops, white with snow, their chimneys black and smoking.

George counted the houses twice and said with satisfaction: 'Cousin Len's not feeling the pinch this week. See how the snow's melted round his chimney.'

Distant yellow windows looked cosy in this black and white world, where an icy wind sliced the air. The boys could hear it rushing across the hill above their heads, gathering to a whistle and then sinking down. In a lull an owl hooted sweetly from the churchyard trees.

George said: 'Wouldn't it be great to take off from this step like a bird? Think of flying on the wind, letting it swing you, like on waves.'

'You ever seen the sea?' Polak asked.

'Only on film.'

'Sometimes I think I'll be a sailor after all.'

'Aye—you're good on ropes.'

Polak was not sure whether this was meant as sarcasm. He pressed the box onto a projecting stone with his hip and considered what he would do in the world. He would do more than the others. He had seen their disappointment following the first excitement of school leaving; the first thrill of holding a job and earning money. He saw how they were trapped in Slidden when they accepted pressure from the Youth Employment Officer, from parents, from pregnant girl friends. The adventure of the great world, of freedom, was a hoax. The only relief for men was drinking in the pub, and wasting money in the betting shop.

'You've always known what you wanted,' he said. 'You're lucky, George.'

George understood. 'I'm not letting them con me. And don't you.'

Polak smiled and nodded in the dark. He thought he would not go into the pits. He lifted the box back onto his head and trudged forward, with George puffing behind, losing way. At the top they turned down an alley and stopped by the back gate of Polak's house.

'You stay here,' Polak whispered, laying the box at his friend's feet.

On the other side over the wall, they could hear Mary Gorman talking to her friend in the garden. The two women were unpegging frost-stiffened nappies from the clothes-line.

65

'Aye, many's the time I've had a terrible beating off him. I says to him only last week, I says, "If we can't come to some decent agreement between us—I'm off!"'

Polak lifted the latch and entered his garden. The rabbit hutch with a sack over its gable was a white hump; the snow, lit from the kitchen window, was pitted with footmarks that led to the door.

How could he best explain? He remembered overhearing Tyotyr tell his mother: 'Always children make more than one excuse when they are lying—remember that, Manya.'

He turned the handle and went in, standing surprised. The kitchen was empty. At once he knew that Tyotyr had left the light on; his mother would never have done such an improvident thing. The kettle was just coming to the boil, just getting up steam to whistle. A tea tray was laid for two, the familiar wobbly tin tray with a scratched picture of a spaniel puppy looking over a brick wall. Quickly Polak shifted the kettle to one side, turned down the gas and stepped softly upstairs to his back bedroom. The sisters shared the large front room. He could hear their voices in the lounge talking Polish.

'There's a draught somewhere.'

'Kettle's a long time boiling.'

'Gas pressure must be poor.'

'We haven't had Mary Gorman in borrowing this week. She must have got the housekeeping off him.'

Two blankets and the flock patchwork quilt Polak took, laying back the cotton coverlet smoothly, so nothing should be noticed. Then he crept down again. He smiled as he imagined his aunt's wailing cry of astonishment when she came in and found the kettle put to one side.

The scrape of chair legs on the lounge lino warned him. Because Tyotyr was fat and had to squeeze between the furniture, there was just time to escape.

Out in the alley he made George help fold the covers into a tidy bundle before setting off for the Trapp.

'I'm shocking hungry,' George said. 'How about testing out the biscuits?'

'I dursn't,' Polak replied. 'Once started there'd be no stopping me. Best wait.'

They trudged out of town, the snow growing whiter and whiter. At the church gate George stopped and read: "'The Milk of Human Kindness is——'" The rest was obliterated by the splash of a snowball. 'Is rot,' he added.

'Why do you always read those things?' Polak asked irritated.

'I can't help it—I like reading. I like jokes.'

'You know what, George? They're going to kill you when we get there.'

'What do you mean? I've done nothing,' George expostulated.

'Read it and think again.'

George read and thought in vain.

Polak strode on, saying: 'Maybe you'd best turn back while there's still time.'

George ran to catch up. 'What have I done? I've done nothing!'

'You've gone and forgotten the milk of human kindness to go in our tea.'

George groaned. 'Your jokes! They're not fit for a comic. Anyway you forgot same as I did. What are you getting at me for?'

'Thought you liked jokes,' Polak said.

10

There were changes in the front room since Polak and George had gone and come. More boards had been ripped from the workshop floor and one, balanced on oil drums, made a low bench. Also a pile of splintered plank sprawled in the corner, ready for the night. The room, lit by the spasmodically flickering fire, was a little warm at last.

Immediately they arrived with food, Lucy took over the cooking. In her eagerness to play the female role she thought the boys expected of her, she remained unaware of the offence it gave to Shem.

Again baked beans, like succulent pink pebbles, and eggs, toadflax yellow, scrambled in Lucy's portable frying pan. There was the argument about how best to keep the fire going, the kettle boiling, the eager muddle of six hungry people. At last the beans and eggs were piled dripping onto slices of bread, handed round, and there was silence.

Lucy's face had turned red in the heat and excitement, her hair hung in curly straggles round her cheek, so that she had to keep brushing it back with her forearm. She had removed her fur jacket and wore a rough blue jersey and tight jeans that showed off her long legs. She gazed at the boys with maternal satisfaction.

Christopher showed no obvious interest. He caressed his

drooping moustache between mouthfuls and his face wore a pinched, startled look. It was certainly a less handsome, less bold face than his sister's, only when he smiled it appeared genuinely kinder. Once he nudged Lucy in a friendly way. Polak noticed and wondered what special meaning this conveyed.

Outside a storm of wind and snow raged.

Christopher finished eating, smiled, leant back and yawned an enormous yawn. Es watched the black hairs, fire-lit under his chin, shift as the skin stretched and contracted.

'It's good to feel your belly tight again,' Christopher gasped, taking off his glasses, squeezing his eyes shut and putting the glasses on again.

Lucy rose and fetched the guitar from where it lay against the rucksack. She unzipped the canvas case and handed the instrument to her brother. He moved across to the plank bench and placed his foot on the end, bending over, watching fingers that were barely visible in the gloom. His figure looked younger, more relaxed. The notes came clear and single, like drops of water, a hiccupping rhythm, a soulful tune, with a chord at the end of each phrase like a splash.

'That what you call Spanish type?' Shem asked, keen to show off his knowledge.

'Sort of Spanish type,' Lucy said, smiling.

A burning board fell out of the grate, spraying white ash and red cinders. Together Lucy and Polak started forward and bumped shoulders.

'Look out, that's hot!' Lucy said.

They put the board back. Polak rammed it into the fire with his heel. Lucy brushed the ashes towards the hearth with a piece of newspaper. He gazed at her hand: a soft, pale, elegantly shaped hand that had not scrubbed floors or wrung sheets. Lucy glanced back with a warm smile. It shocked and excited him.

Christopher had begun to sing. His voice was unaffected

and colourless. Each line moved rhythmically to the strum-ming tune, each word was clear and simple.

> ' When we came,
> when we came
> the snow was falling on the moor.
> Oh God it was cold—
> face all stiff,
> fingers numb,
> toes ten sticks of pain—pain—
> when we came.

> They hauled us up,
> they hauled us in
> to warm by the manufactory fire,
> to melt the pack of ice on my back.
> Oh God that was fine.
> Feet blazed,
> cheek burnt
> when we came.

> And—and—
> and by that fire
> they fed us rosy red baked beans
> when we came—'

Laughter drowned the rest, so he concluded with a series of chords.

Es leapt up, exclaiming: 'You ought to be in a group!'

Lucy said: 'Yes, I always tell him it's unusual to be able to reel it off like that. I'm sure the old troubadours com-posed poetry off the cuff.'

'He ought to be in a group,' Es repeated.

'I've no voice. No——' Christopher laid down the guitar.

'She's the performer—she's the one. She sings in pubs and places. Do you mind if I boast for you, Lu?'

The boys turned to Lucy.

'Are you trad or folk?' George asked.

'I'm nothing,' she said. 'I just sing songs that appeal to me. All sorts.'

'Come on, give us a tune, luv!' Shem said cheekily.

But Lucy shook her head, wiping her fingers fastidiously on her jeans. 'Sometime—not now. I'm dead tired. We walked a long way today.'

'Come on—just a little one!'

Polak considered this insistence unmannerly. He stepped close in front of Shem, blocking him from view.

He said to Christopher: 'It's a mill, not a manufactory. They used to spin yarn here.'

'What's the difference between a factory and a mill?' asked Christopher.

The boys were puzzled.

Es shot up his hand, as though in school. 'Mill's a place where you make—aye—aye—so are factories.' He subsided and they all laughed.

'Well done, our Es!' Shem cried.

'I don't know either, Es,' Lucy said.

'If you think about factories,' George began slowly, 'that's where they manufacture something out of all different kinds of stuff—if you get my meaning. Like take this waistcoat of mine: there's worsted and metal and cotton and canvas. All sorts. Now for milling, you take one thing, like corn or wool—and you change corn into flour and wool into yarn. Right? You don't alter the substance.'

Lucy tore a narrow rectangle from one of the grocery bags and laid a trail of tobacco. 'You forgot my papers, Polak. Why don't you talk more?'

Polak met her eyes. They appeared to be laughing at him. He did not answer, nonplussed and offended.

Es hastened to defend his hero. 'Polak don't say much, but he thinks—you can see him thinking.'

'You must have X-ray eyes,' Shem mocked.

Again they laughed.

Es went to inspect Lucy's cigarette. 'That's a poor lanky wee thing. Looks like your baby brother's legs, George. Let's have a go.'

'Here you are,' Lucy replied equably. She watched him scatter tobacco on the floor. 'He's making the other leg. Who wants a cigarette?'

All refused except Shem. Polak glared, for he considered it ill-mannered to accept anything more from the strangers.

'My folk come from London too,' Shem said, drawing on the cigarette, wishing to establish his alliance with the southerners. He turned to Christopher. 'Don't you smoke?'

Lucy interposed: 'He got put off by his big sister.'

'Perfectly disgusting habit,' Christopher said.

'You young men are so puritanical,' Lucy cried. 'Just listen to him—with his oriental music and his living in the mind! No smoking, no drinking, no nothing.' She looked round at her audience, wondering how old they were, how much she could say.

Christopher spoke quietly: 'So what? The mind is the one interesting and original thing about man. All his other functions are better demonstrated in animals. My aim is to find out what's important in life. There's not enough time for messing around.'

George leant forward. 'How do you mean, better demonstrated in animals?'

'Like—well, like animals have senses better adapted to their needs. Look at that beast.' He pointed to Fleabag, who sat washing his face, the side of his paw licked and then curled over and wiped down his cheek. He washed the same area again and again. 'And look at the way they produce their young—a hundred times more efficient. I mean, just

72

think of the female body! Just look at it!' He spoke with terrible scorn, turning to stare at his sister.

It was with embarrassment that the boys followed his command, and then glanced away.

Christopher continued: 'Whoever designed that pelvis for producing babies ought to be shot. Designed by an amateur—shocking job! And then the spine—unfit to bear the weight of the upright body. As for feet—think of old women's feet!' He had worked himself up into an angry ferment: his moustache and beard bristled and he held his audience triumphantly. 'Designs may look very pretty on paper and be perfectly useless for any practical purpose.' All at once he relapsed, placing his palms against his cheeks and gazing at the floor.

George was excited. 'What about instincts?'

Christopher did not reply.

His sister pushed back her hair and replied: 'I often wonder about my brother's instincts.'

Christopher glanced up annoyed. 'You're always so personal, Lucy. You're intolerable!' Then he put his head back between his hands.

Polak spoke, calmly amused. 'I see you two have had this argument before.'

Lucy smiled. 'Of course we have. But we haven't come to blows—well, not lately.'

There was silence. The six figures were black mounds round the fire, with foreheads and noses small areas of light. When the wood flickered and blazed their faces and hands showed golden, gathering detail as the light increased, disappearing as it faded.

'Wind's up,' Shem remarked at last. 'Must be doing a ton.'

'Sounds more like a thousand miles an hour,' Es said.

George said: 'It's like a woman crying on and on.'

The wind now blew with inward gusts that seemed to

73

press out the surface bulk of sound, until it burst into a great hissing whistle. Then the blast would sink away, only to be followed by another build-up, with the air again swirling and raging as though trapped inside some enormous bag. Gusts, forced into the chimney, whined and hummed up and down the scale, while every so often an enormous huff of smoke would bellow forth into the room. Behind the main roar there were refined, wistful strains, a sharp delicate singing that drove through the air on another level. All these waves of noise were unevenly spaced. There were monstrous sweeping rages and then a sharp silence that came as a shock, then off again on the confused race.

George thought of his problems. He compared his life with Christopher's. 'You're right about the mind. Only some of us don't have the chance. You happen to be one of the lucky ones.'

'So are you, man, if you want to be,' Christopher retorted. 'You've everything: the stones on the road are yours to study, the clever blokes, the stupid ones, libraries, cinema techniques, sex-ridden schoolgirls, snow. You can learn from the simple as well as the complicated. Unfortunately I'm out of touch with the facts of life, like getting food and clothes, like stealing and hitting. I am cut off by the soggy cushion of a middle-class upbringing. You're one up on me.'

'Is that why you came north?' Polak asked.

'Maybe.'

George was excited. 'You talk as though you needed some excuse like—and we don't.'

The young man raised his hand and saluted George across the dusky space.

'And how about her?' Shem asked. 'How about our Lucy?'

Lucy began eagerly: 'I wanted to escape from London, because—because of personal reasons.' She seemed to regret her frankness half way through the sentence.

74

'Boy friend trouble?' Shem said with his cheeky lilt.

Polak did not like this conversation.

The brother turned back to George. 'She's quite a clever girl in some ways. She can pass exams like a bomb. But oh, the terrible thing of being female!'

Es expostulated: 'She can't help it, poor thing!'

So they laughed, except for Polak.

A flame shot up in the grate and Lucy met his eyes. Her face flushed red. She could not tell whether he saw this or not, but his eyes remained fixed on her.

Es yawned a huge sighing moan, his mouth as wide as the gaping beak of a young bird. Polak fetched blankets from the corner.

'You'd best lay down, Es,' he said.

At this Lucy also brought her bedding roll into the circle and they began to prepare for sleep.

Fleabag, disturbed, was trying to open the door.

'Where does one pee?' Lucy asked her brother.

'Female problems——'

'Toilet's downstairs,' Polak said. 'I'll show you.'

They took the precious candle to light the way. The lavatory was not used because there was no water. It was more convenient for the boys to pee out of the store-room windows, always hoping, as Shem said, to douse the Bullman gang and kill two birds with one stone.

Polak waited in the dark outside, having warned Lucy about the poles.

'It's nice to be escorted,' she said, emerging and handing back the candle. 'Two hundred years ago gallants also escorted their ladies to the privy.'

Her remark embarrassed him. He tripped on the fallen balustrade and stumbled against her. A froth of hair brushed his face, candle grease burnt his hand, the flame jerked and went out.

'Sorry,' he gasped.

He stretched his arm to feel for the wall.

'Best take my hand. I know the way.'

Lucy smiled, wondering whether he had put out the candle on purpose. She wondered whether he would try to kiss her, and was half disappointed, half relieved that he did not.

Upstairs Christopher had arranged his sister's bed. They were to sleep in a semicircle round the fire: he at one end, Lucy next, then Es.

'You'd better close up,' he advised. 'We're going to freeze.'

Es suggested: 'Anyone who wakes put wood on the fire—or it'll be out by morning.'

'Right, lads!' Shem said. 'That kid has more sense than you'd think. He won't be the one to wake.'

The boys spread newspaper on the floor and then laid a blanket on top.

'This is a shocking hard mattress,' Shem commented.

Lucy advised: 'You'd better put the quilt to lie on, and have a blanket between each pair—it's a rule of keeping warm—to have as much underneath as on top.'

She unbuckled her belt and tugged off her boots, then wriggled into her sleeping-sack. Sitting up she took her fur jacket and laid it half over Es, who lolled beside her.

'Come on, snuggle up, Es! You look a real cherub.'

Polak stretched beside Es. Shem was waiting for George.

'That's right, darling. Take off your boots and come into my arms!'

Polak tucked the blanket under his legs, speaking severely: 'You lay still, Esmond Cattermole, and don't squirm.'

'When I say turn, we all turn,' Shem said.

'Hey, you've pulled all the blanket over your side!' George cried.

And so, fidgeting and trying not to fidget, pressed against each other, they fell asleep.

11

Polak woke in the grey before dawn and did not know where he was. He felt a lump under his ribs like a log of wood and, trying to drag it out, discovered that it was his own arm gone dead. The arm was hard, cold, senseless: an obstinate weight that would not budge, so he turned on his back and began to pinch and massage the flesh. As he rubbed, fearful the limb would never again revive, he remembered why he was on a hard floor, why his toes hurt with cold, why the air smelt sharp and dusty, why the ceiling, faintly lightened by a reflection of snow, dripped and looped with monstrous cobweb streamers.

Then his arm began to tingle, softly at first, but accelerating with more and more intensity, till the limb was a seething mass of sensation. He drew in his breath to restrain a grunt. Es stirred. At this Polak remembered how Lucy had lain on the other side of Es all night. Had he slept less heavily he might have pushed Es over and got in between. Making up the fire could have been an excuse.

He raised himself on one elbow. The fire was very low, a few red embers glowing palely amid a sea of white ash. It must be made up. Quietly he slithered out and filled the grate with wood, which soon began to flare and crackle. In this new light he turned to inspect the place he had restrained himself from looking at till now, as though it was a treat to be saved till last. He peered across the rumpled, humped blankets to where the girl's sleeping-sack spread, and he saw that it was flat and empty.

Then he inspected the room with care. There was her brother's black hair sprouting from the top of his sleeping-bag and the length of his body outlined. There was Es with an expression of pained surprise on his round forehead, his knees drawn up, dirt on his mouth. Shem lay on his back, his lips that were usually twisted into some sort of grimace, now open and relaxed; his sharp nose pointed straight at the ceiling as he snored gently. George had hunched himself against the cold, his back pressed into Shem's side, his legs stuck out from the blankets with heels and toes peering whitely from shrivelled torn socks; he had hidden his face in his arm, as though to protect it from a blow. And there was her place, empty.

Polak gazed into the shadow. She was gone. It was a disaster he had never anticipated.

Next it occurred to him that she might have left the room in order to pee. This seemed logical. Her coat was gone and her boots. He stood, warming his back at the fire, and waited for the sound of footsteps. Nothing. He waited and waited. Not even the wind stirred round the Trapp on this winter morning. There was silence.

'I'll go daft like this,' Polak muttered.

He tiptoed over and found his boots. The leather laces were frosted stiff. He did not notice when one cut his finger. His mind was obsessed with the question: why, where had she gone?

First he went to the lavatory and clambered among the poles, searching in the farthest stall in case she had fallen or fainted. The door he had jammed across the window was in place, so she could not have escaped that way. Every moment his anxiety increased, till he had wild visions of a Bullman gang kidnapping.

There was no one in the little office, or in the great workshop, where an icy draught rustled the straw. Through the barred windows he saw the snow lay thick across the undulating moor. Above the horizon thin bars of black cloud streaked the sky, that was now fading from grey to white.

Polak mounted the stair. It might be that he would have to go out in search of her. How had they lured her away? He would kill them if they had? At the thought of battle his strength swelled and he felt himself invincible, like a mythical hero. He pictured a fine struggle and the rescue of Lucy.

There came a sound and he stopped. Five single notes rang from a distance across the hollow hall, like glowing marbles. In a moment he guessed and leapt, three steps at a time.

Lucy had opened one of the doors on the loading bay. She sat on an oil drum, her leather coat splayed over her, silhouetted against the sky that was now pink, with the streaks of black cloud a rust colour on their under side, every moment absorbing more and more orange light.

Although the door to the store-room grated, Lucy did not hear, she was so intent on watching the outer world. Her fingers plucked the guitar strings automatically and she pressed the instrument into her body as though to keep it warm.

Polak leant against the wall just inside the door, watching, listening. From where he stood she was framed against the sky and hills. He did not wish to disturb the picture.

Lucy played evenly, softly, as the world outside changed colour. The sun, still hidden, sent up an arc of fiery red light that sprayed out from the farthest hill; the upper sky was white, fading to egg-shell blue where a faint star shone. The once black clouds were now a raw and angry red all round their edges, while the snow below glowed orange and crimson, as though some battle had taken place that night and left its stain.

As the colour intensified Lucy played more loudly, with

more chords. She rocked her body back and forth on the oil drum and at one moment laughed, ending in a curious sob. At length the edge of the sun mounted above the hill, a flaring arc that sent a shaft across the snow, and immediately the red faded and the world turned gold. Half the sun and then the whole circle came swimming out into the sky, as though loosened from a mooring. Snow now glinted brilliant white on the uplands, while in the western valleys sweeping horizontal shadows, a deep blue colour, stretched into every dip and dell.

Lucy sang once the sun was free, each first line on a bold rising scale, the second in a minor key, descending. Her voice was clear and rich, with a silky simplicity that contrasted with the fanciful accompaniment. She was plainly composing the words as she went along, for at moments she hesitated or stopped playing altogether. She was not a smart improviser like her brother.

'Sun—sun—sun—
Solnitza—solnitza—solnitza—
Sol—sol—sol—
Soleil—soleil—soleil—
Sonne—sonne—sonne—
Sole—o sole—o sole.'

The verse was repeated a second time with confidence, her voice sounding more polished. She stopped and, turning, looked along the shaft of sunlight that now cut across the room, with Polak standing at the end.

'Hallo—good morning!' she said, shaking back her hair.

Polak walked over and stood on the sill, gazing down at sunlit Lucy. Her cheeks were golden pink, like a peach, and the dirty grey wool that lined her coat was creamy and bright. The strings of the guitar sparkled silver, the wood shone sweet and delicate.

'I didn't know where you'd gone,' he said.

She raised her face and their eyes met, Lucy's enormous brown eyes and Polak's grey slanted eyes. His mouth fell a little open, while Lucy flushed almost as crimson as the snow before sunrise. Polak could not bear her affectionate gaze and jerked his head away towards the moor. Along the horizon a load of mauve cloud was rising. They spoke together.

'That was——'

'You shouldn't——'

'Go on,' she said.

'It doesn't matter,' he replied.

Lucy said in a husky voice: 'See how fast that cloud gathers. It's going to overtake the sun.'

'Most like that'll be the last we'll see of the sun today. There's more snow to come; that's for sure.'

'It's so strange up here in the north. So lonely. I like the stone, the black and the white.'

They watched the cloud bank piling up and up, armed with darkness, till it covered the sun. The snow wastes at once turned grey.

Then Lucy handed Polak her guitar and stiffly, stretching and kicking her legs, rubbing her mauve-white knuckles, stood up.

'Do you see, we're the same height?' she said, and touched the sleeve of his jacket.

He was not pleased to be the same height. He wanted to be taller, but her hand on his arm made his spirit leap. He could not speak.

'Shall we make breakfast?'

'We'll need snow for tea,' Polak said. 'I'll fetch the kettle and we'll take it fresh off the ledge.'

He carried the guitar back to the front room and returned with the kettle, which they packed with snow.

'Press it down firm,' he said. 'It shrinks something shocking when it melts.'

'Are you English?' Lucy asked as they bent together and she studied the line of his cheek.

'Nay, I'm Polish.'

'I thought you were an interesting colour as soon as I saw you. And is Polak your real name?'

The boy stood up straight as though on parade. 'My father's name was Stanislav Stiletski, but he changed that when he knew he couldn't go back, after the war. I'm Eugene Polak—Gene Polak they call me.'

'What does your father do? Does he work in the mines or——'

'My Dad's dead. But maybe I'll be going into the pits—haven't made up my mind yet.' He paused and added: 'He was a dancer. He came over here in the war to fight——' Polak rubbed the palms of his hands together and the dirt dripped off, wet with snow.

'A Polish dancer—how marvellous!' Lucy exclaimed. 'Can you—can you dance the mazurka?'

'Course he can!' answered Es, coming into the store-room. 'And he can do acrobatics—all sorts. He's learning me. We'll have a double act before long, won't we, Polak? Let's show Lucy!'

'Not before breakfast,' Polak replied sharply. 'Come on, young Es, you take this kettle and see to the fire.'

12

After breakfast they slid down the rope into the snow, with the intention of collecting coal from a slag heap. Polak carried the cardboard box. They ran to keep warm, floundering in holes and shouting.

'It feels like I've been let out of prison!' Es called, leaping over a mound.

Lucy's hair flopped up and down on her shoulders and she laughed, but did not scream like the girls they were accustomed to. Chased by Es she fell over a hummock and sat in the snow with pink shining cheeks and nose.

'If we were in Poland,' she said, gazing across the whiteness, 'there would be the tracks of wolves and little cleft hoof marks of wild boar in the snow.'

'Why pick on Poland?' her brother asked.

'His family comes from there.' She nodded towards Polak.

The boys gathered round. She sat so long they thought she must be hurt.

'You'll get a numb bum,' Shem said.

Lucy rose obediently, remarking: 'What we need is a shovel. And that box of yours isn't going to be much use: the bottom'll fall out when it gets damp.'

'Shall we go over to the tip?' George the scavenger asked. 'We might find a bucket and spade. It's good fun there.'

Christopher objected that the tip would be deep in snow, but George explained it faced south-west, while the wind was driving from the north-east.

'Isn't it fine the way they all know the lie of the land and the way the wind blows up here?' Lucy said.

Christopher added: 'In London we're such ignorant bastards no one knows which is south or north. But here north, south, east and west have their own character, their own meaning in your lives. One grows aware of one's relation to the Pole Star and the continent where Russia lies, and China beyond.'

'My brother speaks with such authority everyone listens. Isn't he lucky? That's why he'll be a good journalist.' Lucy was mocking and at the same time admiring.

'You're brother's the romantic type,' George replied, feeling himself akin.

They trudged contentedly.

'I believe that it's being isolated makes you more perceptive. Your heads aren't all cluttered up with clichés.'

George spoke. 'I tell you, us poor folk—we think about the destiny of man much more than folk with washing machines and flowers up the front path. I mean, everyone wants something to worry about.'

'Oh, that's cutting!' Lucy cried.

George's face crumpled in a bitter pained expression; he jerked his head on his shoulders several times, like a puppet. He felt irritated by the silly girl.

'You're always taking the mickey out of someone, aren't you,' he said.

Lucy felt ashamed of herself. She ran on ahead, mounting an incline, and turned to face her companions. She called down to her brother: 'Isn't it marvellous? Now aren't you glad I made you run away from London? We would never have known the Trapp, or the moors, or the snow. Aren't you glad now?' She lifted one arm and turned up her head in the position of an angel in St Chad's churchyard, showing off her handsome legs. 'And look! The sun's coming out again. Polak said it wouldn't.'

There was a break in the clouds and she stood sunlit.

Christopher followed George over the edge of the tip, that dropped down in a cliff of rubbish.

But Polak bounded up beside the girl. They surveyed the white undulating desert, the Trapp half hidden. Telegraph poles standing black along a distant road to the south, stunted trees bent before the weather, stone walls, lumpish and shadowed, leading the eye for miles up and down.

'What's that?' Lucy asked, pointing to the pair of iron wheels perched on a scaffold, whose thin spokes were turning.

'That's for the pit. That's Grimsgill Colliery,' Polak replied, surprised at her ignorance.

'And Slidden behind us,' she said.

Polak turned to see St Chad's tower and beyond the black chimneys: the place where he lived.

'Aye. I wonder will Slidden ever be behind me?'

'Perhaps one day I'll come to work in your hospital. I wouldn't mind working here in the north.'

'And when I'm brought in from the pit on a stretcher I shall look up and say: "Ee—Dr Lucy!"' He stared at her aggressively, exaggerating his north country accent. 'That won't half choke you and your fancy manners and being different and all!'

Lucy opened her big eyes at him, hurt, surprised. Then she stepped down, following the indented path the others had left. Polak came after, upset.

They crossed a strand of sagging barbed wire where a board was nailed to the post with an almost obliterated notice: 'No Tipping. Trespassers will be Prosecuted'. They stumbled on uneven ground to the verge of the ragged promontory. A gulley made by rain led the way down, where scroungers over many years had trespassed. Here, as George foretold, the slope was almost clear of snow, which only settled on objects that protruded from the general mass. There were food tins, newspapers, oil drums, pram wheels, plastic containers, a pink striped mattress, ashes, things grey and black, all soaked soft with time and weather. There was a stench of rotting cabbage and burning horse hair and mildew.

Lucy was disgusted, but restrained herself in deference to those who took the place for granted as a source of benefits. She paused half way, unwilling to sink her boots farther into the stinking slush. Below figures moved about, taking up and discarding the varied offerings. There was an echoing clang as Shem hurled a bottle at a piece of corrugated iron.

Es's voice came up clear and cheerful: 'Look what I've found—bloody great coal scuttle!'

'Aye, but bottom's knocked out.'

Es chucked it aside.

They watched Christopher step over a bedstead and retrieve the scuttle, shaking out the snow.

'You could wedge a bit of metal and it would do fine.'

Voices echoed against the cliff.

Polak stood behind Lucy. 'Let's go down,' he said.

She squeezed aside, tottering on a tuft of red and blue rags that crackled as icy particles were crushed.

'I'll wait at the top. It smells.' She could not conceal her revulsion.

Polak brushed by. He thought she was scorning more than mere smells.

When at length they were tired of the tip, they moved on to the nearest slag heap, armed with part of a fender and pieces of board with which to scrape away snow and dig. The scuttle, whose bottom was now restored by a piece of bent tin, was soon full of the hard shaley coal. Then the cardboard box was filled.

From the tip Es had unearthed two cups with which he

was delighted. One was large and white with a gold clover leaf on the side, the other pink with red roses all round; neither had a handle, but they were only chipped, not cracked. When Lucy made a face, Es wiped them with snow. She said they should be sterilized with boiling water.

It was freezing cold, the leaden sky hung depressingly low, The time had come when they were all looking forward to the protection of the Trapp and hot tea.

With a burst of energy Es ran ahead. George and Christopher carried the scuttle between them and conversed.

George said: 'I've been noticing that folk who write—even a decent teacher—they'll use symbols, no, metaphors to make something clear. Do you see what I mean? I mean, those who just talk about the thing itself are that dry you can't concentrate.'

Christopher said: 'In fact, one understands best via the imagination.'

'Aye, that's right. But what puzzles me is—why can't you just rely on the logic of the mind? Human beings are that stupid and that clever——'

'Yes, the human mind requires amusing—the excitement of a good metaphor.' He gave his ironic grin.

'Our old Mac—he's headmaster—he's always going on about "life's a metaphor". But they don't care. They don't listen.'

'Hey—let's change round. My arm aches.'

They put down the scuttle and switched sides.

George went doggedly back to his question. 'Sometimes I wonder if it isn't just ignorance. That poet called Marlowe, he said,

"'I count religion but a childish toy,
And hold there is no sin but ignorance."

'That stuck in my mind.'

Christopher stopped. 'Here, put this thing down. So you do read.'

'There you go—you don't half sound patronizing.'

They stood waiting for the others to catch up.

Seeing Christopher discomforted, George went on : 'You're ever so sure of yourself, Christopher, aren't you?'

When Shem, Lucy and Polak came up, Christopher addressed them with self-conscious enthusiasm. 'This has been a most satisfactory expedition: a scuttle, coal to go in the scuttle, half a fender to go round them and two cups. All free of charge. There's no doubt one prizes necessities when they are scarce.'

'Get moving, George,' Shem said.

'Of course, there are too many things in the world,' Christopher continued. 'Everywhere man-made junk cluttering it up! I like the idea of using a little of what we've got, rather than demanding more and more. Come to think of it, this island will soon be nothing more than a big pile of rusting motor-cars and plastic containers. Men are disgusting creatures!'

The boys listened.

Shem said to Lucy : 'Economical bloke, your brother.'

She smiled. 'I've never noticed it before. But necessity brings out hidden genius.'

'Sarcastic cow!' Christopher exclaimed over his shoulder.

Lucy did not like being spoken to thus in front of the boys. She snapped back: 'Sorry! We don't all have to take your pomposities seriously!'

The Slidden lads were curious to witness a squabble between these aliens. It was not a bit like their family rows.

Christopher thumped down his side of the scuttle and turned to face his sister. 'If ever I show the least—but the least sign of breaking away from your pattern of behaviour, the pattern you have decided is right, I'm "puritan" or "pompous" or "exhibitionist" or "a genius". I'm anything you can think up in the way of sly abuse.'

'My God, I was only laughing at you a little. One must be allowed to laugh at people. And necessity does bring out genius. Look at these boys——'

Polak squatted in the snow, scooping up coal that had spilt. He glanced from Lucy's excited face to the brother, who wore a look of sulky fury.

At this moment Es appeared running round a pyramid of shale, running as fast as the snow would allow.

'Quick!' he gasped. 'They're getting in. Red's half way up the rope!'

Without a word the boys dropped their burdens and ran. Lucy stood watching. Es, already puffed, lagged behind. They were all soon out of sight behind the slag heap. With some difficulty Lucy hoisted and wedged the cardboard box under her left arm and with her right lifted the coal bucket. Slowly she trudged after.

The Trapp soon came into full view. The door on the loading bay was open, just as it had been left and the rope hung, swinging back and forth. The five boys were plunging through the snow, Christopher and Polak ahead, bent dark figures that seemed to have difficulty in lifting their feet.

Arrived, Polak went to look round the corner of the building, in case of an ambush. Shem came up and they stood together, consulting.

Lucy staggered on. Once she stopped to rest and shift her burdens. She saw her brother take hold of the knotted end of the rope. They still talked. To her relief he stood back as Polak sprang. The boy jack-knifed his way up easily and deliberately. Es bent and pressed a snowball hard in his hands. His voice came across the distance.

'I'll have this ready, in case he comes out and attacks.'

'Look out you don't hit me instead,' Polak called down.

Everyone gazed anxiously at the platform.

Polak made his way to the top like a monkey on a stick. No enemy appeared to knock him down again. At the end of the rope he paused to gather strength, swung his body and flung it over the sill. He scrambled to his feet and disappeared into the Trapp.

Christopher came to meet Lucy. He carried the scuttle to the grey patch of stamped ice round the rope.

Shem fixed Es with a sharp stare. 'Seeing Red on that rope—maybe it was your imagination.'

Es turned pink. 'It weren't! I did! He were half way up!'

'Maybe he was coming down.'

'He—he weren't!' Es cried angrily. Then a twinge of anxiety crossed his smooth face and he began to doubt his memory. 'I mean to say, I think he were.'

George stamped his wet feet and groaned, 'Oh, my chil-blains!' gazing up at the platform and grimacing.

They all stamped as they waited. The sensation of half-frozen fingers and toes was spiteful, behind the sharper pain a heavy ache.

Then George stood still, his head on one side. 'Listen!'

'Didn't I tell you?' Es whispered, terrified but triumphant.

'I'm going,' Christopher said.

'Beware they don't jump you round a corner. And don't say I didn't warn you,' Shem mocked.

There was a nervous whine in Es's voice. 'It's like—you know, it's like them fairy stories where one goes in and never comes out. So the next goes in and doesn't come out. And then the next goes to find what's become of him—and you know——'

'Till last of all,' George continued, 'the youngest one goes in, tricks the lot of them and marries the princess.'

'Don't be daft!' Es cried irritably.

'I'd better go and see,' Christopher said to Lucy.

He started up the rope slowly.

Es jigged about, shouting the advice of his PT master.

'Hold your breath, lad! Take it easy—make yourself light. Cross those feet more. Go on—grip with your feet.'

Half way Christopher paused and gasped: 'I'll just take a look round and let you know if all's well.'

He went on awkwardly, drawing breath in loud gulps. At the top it seemed he would never reach the platform, for his arm caught on the edge of the sill feebly and his body trembled, leaning out from the rope over the abyss.

Lucy watched with open mouth, tense and terrified.

Christopher grasped, slipped and grasped again. Then he was on the sill, legs kicking. He crawled away into the store-room.

Lucy let out her breath.

Christopher reappeared and waved.

'It looks OK! I'll go find Polak!' he called and dis-appeared.

'You look out!' Es cried.

13

When Polak first stood alone in the store-room he waited and listened. There was the sound of steps below, distant and diminishing. He sped to the door and peered. Nothing. He crept to the landing and looked into the front room.

The front room was in havoc. Lucy's guitar lay splintered in the middle of the floor. Blankets were scattered, no longer in the neat pile where Christopher had folded them. A sleeping-sack, stuffed into the fire, smouldered and filled the air with the acrid stench of burnt feathers.

Polak immediately pulled this out and stamped on the glowing hole. He noted the kettle beside the wall in a pool of water. The contents of the rucksack had been emptied and scattered: socks, comb, books, shirt torn. Spilt biscuits made a yellow heap on the hearth. The bench was knocked over, the mug smashed.

Again Polak ground the burning feathers under his boot and his eyes returned to the guitar. Its back had been smashed in, the polished wood split and torn apart. The neck had snapped, but was still attached to the body by one string, while others lay curling in the dust. His mind contracted with rage. He could not bear to look any more.

Then, with the surge of anger still rising, Polak sped downstairs. He knew it was pointless to try to go silently: the echo of boots on stone must warn any intruder. So he ran steadily, every sense alert. First he chose to search the office, and had just found it empty when Fleabag's ferocious hiss sounded from across the hall. He emerged to see the cat race out of the shop and upstairs, with Red in close pursuit, brandishing a six-foot pole and yelling:

'I'll get you—you devil!'

Polak followed, but his boot slipped on something wet and he fell, striking his head on the bottom step. As he struggled slowly to his feet, half stunned, he saw a trail of blood leading up the stairs and knew that Fleabag had struck. Swaying and fighting to keep balance, Polak climbed, while from above came a shout, the clang of metal, a crash, another shout and thumping boots.

When Polak at last reached the store-room door, he saw Fleabag at bay on the platform, facing his enemy with ears laid back, eyes bulging, and the hair all over his body bristling like a chimney brush. Red was advancing warily, the pole extended before him, as the cat hissed and spat.

'Out of my way!' Red cried to the cat. 'Let me by!'

'You dare! You dare!' shouted Polak.

He rushed forward, so that Red had hardly time to turn before Polak grappled his arm and the pole fell to the floor with an echoing clang. Then they tumbled together, gasping and struggling, bitter and vicious, fighting to gain the upper hand.

Red and Polak were well matched in strength and cunning, but Polak was very angry, Red on the defensive. So they rolled and kicked and twisted, until Polak finally struggled on top, smothering his victim, and began to push him nearer and nearer to the drop over the loading bay.

When Red felt his feet wave in the air he fought desperately to save himself. He clutched at the edge of the door, while the weight of his legs hanging unsupported dragged him over the ledge. He gasped from underneath Polak's stomach in a strangled voice:

'Stop—stop, Polak! I'm going! Stop!'

Polak, engulfed in a spasm of fury, hardly knew what he did or what he wished to do. But the cry brought him to his senses. He stopped and staggered upright.

Red slowly hauled his legs in, rolled over and knelt, looking up apprehensively. His flaming hair was tousled, his pinky-mauve skin and clothes smeared with dirt, a bruise was beginning to show on his cheek, while the back of his right hand dripped blood from three deep claw marks. The seam of his jacket had split round one armhole.

Polak had a cut beneath his hair, from which a stream of blood ran down the side of his face, also a great bump on his forehead. One eye was half closed where Red had tried to gouge it. His collar was torn from the shirt and hung down at the back.

'You!' Polak said with furious intensity. 'Get off, you! And you'd best not come near me again—ever!'

Red scrambled and leapt for the rope, sliding into the midst of his enemies so suddenly that he almost escaped. But in a moment Shem and George had a firm hold, while Polak landed immediately after.

'You've something to answer for!' Polak cried, still beside himself with rage. 'You smashed her guitar! You done it deliberate.'

Red stared down and did not speak.

'What shall we do to him?' Shem asked.

'No!' cried Lucy. 'No—don't!'

'Why not?' Shem demanded, twisting Red's arm ferociously.

Red grimaced and bent over.

'Let him go!' Lucy commanded.

'Red deserves all that's coming to him,' George said huskily.

Polak wiped blood from his eye, threw back his head and a wicked little smile appeared on his lips.

'Aye, she's right,' he said. 'Let him go, lads. He smashed it deliberate and I won't forget that. Never.'

He pushed George aside, gripped Red's wrist and glared at him with eyes half closed, slanting.

'You run along.'

He let go.

Red returned the challenging gaze. He assumed an air of contempt, then turned to Lucy.

'I appreciate what the chick done for me.'

He walked away with dignity, trying to disguise a limp until he was round the corner of the mill. His hand had dripped a trail of blood that left neat red holes in the snow.

Shem and George stood seething with indignation, but Lucy and Es were more concerned at Polak's battered appearance.

Lucy said: 'You nearly killed him. When I saw those boots come over the edge—look, your ear is full of blood.'

Polak leant his head on one side and tried to shake it out, but pain shot behind his eyes.

'Where's Christopher?' Es demanded.

'Aye, where is he?' Polak echoed, looking round at the boys.

'He came in after you.'

'You mean he's up there?'

They nodded.

'Come on then.' His voice told them he was worried.

Polak climbed the rope and Es followed. They went into the store-room, but shortly returned.

'You can make it, Shem. Come on!' Polak called down.

Shem climbed the rope.

'Is he there?' Lucy asked.

'Come on up.'

95

'I don't know if I can manage. Can't you pull me?' Lucy sounded almost tearful. 'What's the matter?'

'Polak's busy,' Es called. 'You have a go.'

Lucy removed her fur jacket and gave it to George. She gathered her strength and sprang. It was a long struggle up the rope and terrifying because of the height, but at last she flopped across the sill to be dragged in.

Polak said: 'He's over there by the door. Don't move him till we come. There's George to haul up first.'

No one expected George to climb the rope.

The room had grown grey. By the far door was a humped shape.

'Christopher! Christopher!' Lucy whispered, feeling for his face.

He took her hand, his hand very cold.

'You have been a long time. I thought you'd all gone off. Something has happened to my leg. I daren't move it. The pain is quite bad.'

'We'll manage. Don't worry,' she reassured him, although inwardly terrified. 'We'll manage—we'll manage.' This repetition was exasperating, yet she could not stop repeating herself. 'They're hauling George in now. I'll fetch a blanket. We'll manage—we'll manage.'

She hurried to the front room and stood aghast at the holocaust: her broken guitar, the pyramid of biscuits, the kettle in its pool of water. She took two blankets, averting her eyes from the guitar, and ran back to her brother, by whom she crouched silently, considering how she, in training to be a doctor, was helpless in this emergency.

There came the sound of the squeaking pulley, Es's high voice, the thump of boots in the bare room.

Christopher groaned.

Again Lucy leant forward and took his hand.

'You've broken your leg, I suppose.'

'I didn't. It was Red,' he replied.

96

14

A stretcher had been improvised. This was done by cutting holes at the bottom corners of the unburnt sleeping-sack and running two six-foot poles through. Christopher was then shifted onto a blanket and so lifted into the centre of the sleeping sack. George and Polak carried him into the front room.

At first, the sight of the havoc wrought by Red unmanned the boys. George stood white and speechless, Es open-mouthed, a caricature of astonishment. Shem poured forth his anger in a stream of words that had none of the usual sarcasm.

'If I'd known what he'd done, I'd have killed him. You knew, Polak. Why didn't you kill him? He deserves it. They're what Chris said—barbarians—right barbarians! I'll give them what for next time, I—just look at that guitar —look at it! If I'd known what he'd done, I'd have killed him! Just look at my mug!'

'Shut your gob!' Polak interrupted. 'Get the place straight. Make up the fire, Es, and save them biscuits. Put on kettle. Get cracking.'

'Why didn't you kick him in——'

'One more word and I'll kick you. Come on, George, don't just stand there gawping. Are you going to let them have the laugh on us?'

So they plucked up courage and cleared. But the heart seemed to have gone out of their home. The stench of singed feathers, the broken guitar, gave a desolate air.

All the while Christopher struggled to hide his pain behind levity. But every forced laugh jarred through Lucy, so that she could hardly bear to stay in the room. However, once the fire began to blaze she squatted beside the stretcher and regained her self-control. Her brother's face was a whitish grey colour, the mouth open, drawing quick shallow breaths. She drew back the blanket and asked for a knife.

Shem produced Red's flick knife and they all stood round as she slit up the front of Christopher's trouser from ankle to thigh.

'What a waste of good jeans!' Es exclaimed.

The tough cotton fitted tight and it was difficult to push the knife through.

'Yes—wicked waste.' Christopher clapped his teeth together. 'Hey—don't drag my leg off, idiot!'

Lucy continued to force the knife with brutal calm.

Suddenly Shem blanched, went to the fire and pushed wood about to make the kettle boil. A kettle more bent and battered than ever, but still more or less watertight.

George felt sick, but could not tear his eyes from the white muscular calf, thickly spread with black hair.

There was, in fact, no bloody wound, only a curious sunken cavity below the knee and a darkening great bruise. It was the awful unnatural position of the lower leg bent sideways that turned the stomach.

'It's odd, to say the least,' Christopher remarked, raising himself on his elbow to look. 'But if they all grew that way one wouldn't——' He shifted to see better and gave a yell. A spasm passed over his face and he lay back with clenched fists.

'Clear up this mess of wood. Make tea,' Polak ordered. 'Lucky you found them cups, Es. George, see if you can't rip up another board below. Right, lads.'

Lucy laid the blanket back over the leg.

'We must get you to hospital somehow. I can't set that.'

Polak asked: 'How about if you took one of them banisters for a splint?'

'I don't know if the knee joint is damaged. You've a hospital in Slidden, haven't you?'

'Aye, there's the hospital. But how's he going to get there? He can't climb out of the Trapp. Unless we break open doors there's no way out. And the doors are that strong.' He rumpled his hair. 'You wouldn't get an ambulance past the church. The road subsided a year since—and what with snow and all——'

'Someone must have a key to this place,' Christopher said.

'Aye!' cried Es. 'Who'll have the key to the gates, Polak?'

'Keys on Sunday night—you're joking!' Shem said. 'It'll be some daft agent like Hacketts.' He tipped water into the teapot.

The room was darkening, the wind rising. They considered the problem. Shem handed round sweet tea, one cup to be shared between three.

'Hey, I got the rosy one!' Es said delighted.

Lucy took the white cup, no longer worried as to whether it had been scalded. She sat cross-legged on a blanket and rocked gently.

Christopher now felt better. He spoke in a cheerful voice. 'It's not bad, so long as I don't move.'

'Go on, then,' George said. 'Give us the grief story.'

Christopher twiddled strands of his beard. 'He did it with one of these.' He touched the metal that protruded from his sleeping-sack. 'It wasn't me he was after, nor Polak: it was that cat——' He spoke jerkily, remembering.

'Fleabag!' Lucy exclaimed.

'It was when Polak was downstairs. I was hiding behind the store-room door. The cat rushed in with Red immediately after. He took a great swipe at it with this pole and missed.

99

The pole swung on and caught me on the leg. It was extra-ordinary—the bone gave a crack like a stick snapping. Red hardly knew what he'd done, he wanted to get away so quick. He gave a sort of startled look and dashed for the rope, but that crazy cat was in the way, spitting like a maniac.'

'Good old Fleabag!' Es cried.

'Then Polak rushed in and tackled him.'

They were silent, munching the crumbled biscuit.

'Where are them cards you said you'd fetch, Shem?' Es asked.

'I forgot.'

'You aren't half a nit.'

Again silence.

After a while Lucy said: 'I wish it didn't grow dark so quickly. Why is this place empty?'

George explained: 'Trapp went bust. There's several more done that round here in the last few years. The machinery was sold for scrap.'

'Have you noticed the way wind gets up every night: it's got into bad habits,' Shem remarked.

'A windy Sunday night and where's the key?' George said.

Es looked at Polak. 'Couldn't we fix the stretcher to the rope some way and let him down? Sort of like a carry-cot.'

Polak did not reply, but he stood up and stretched. 'Come on, lads, we must get cracking. There's doors to be opened.' He led the way out.

Left alone, the brother and sister grinned at each other. It seemed a long time since they had talked together.

'A bit of a mess,' Christopher said.

'They're absolutely sweet.'

'Sweet is hardly the word I'd use.'

'You know what I mean. Only George smells rather.'

'George is bright. Did you see Shem? I thought he was going to faint when he saw my leg.'

'No—I was looking at your leg and feeling sick myself.'

A low thudding sounded. They listened.

'The wind's as bad as last night.'

'Yes, that worries me too. Supposing they do force the door—it's a good mile through the snow, and in the dark. How are they going to carry me that far?'

'I know.'

'We may have to wait till morning, Lu. Anyway I'm safe enough here.'

They were silent again. After a while there more thudding.

Lucy threw wood on the fire, saying: 'It's most peculiar —the Polish one makes me shy.'

Christopher gave a sly grin. 'I know. I saw you blush. You must find him attractive.'

'Oh, but that would be ridiculous—he's so young!'

'To be ridiculous is not unusual, my girl.'

Lucy put on a serious face. She was keen to be honest.

'I wonder? There is something poetic about his—his simplicity, his intelligence—and of course his neck.'

Christopher laughed, stopped short and gasped: 'Bloody hell, what a silly thing to happen!'

15

Below, in the workshop, the boys inspected the ten-foot doors. They were made from massive planks, cross bolted, with hinges that looked as though they had been forged by giants. The centre was fixed top and bottom with bolts which had rusted into their sockets, in the middle was a mortice lock with a two-inch keyhole. Beams had been nailed right across from wall to wall, and these crossed the small wicket door cut into the right-hand gate. This had a Yale lock. It was clear that it would be very difficult to force the doors open without tools.

After studying the problem, they went to the back exit opposite the chimney stack. Shem gave the door a hefty kick, but it hardly trembled.

George remarked: 'A battering ram—that's what they used in the olden days with castles.'

'Hooray for the battering ram!' cried Es.

'Timber's thick as my wrist,' Polak said discouragingly. 'And where's your ram? You want a tree trunk.'

No one answered. Wind rushed against the outside of the mill and spun round the corner, carrying with it a yell.

'Ay—ay—more visitors!' Shem said. 'Didn't know we were that popular.'

With clattering boots they raced up the stairs and opened one of the doors. A group of boys stood below.

'Hey!' yelled Shem, waving.

For answer the air was filled with a shower of snowballs that thudded and clanged.

Polak stamped on one and picked up the contents. 'See that? They put stones in the middle.'

He went onto the platform and held up both hands. There came a howl of excitement from below.

'Stop that, you! We've a lad from London here with a broken leg. You going to help fetch him out?'

Another shower of missiles clattered.

'Come on in, you nutter!' Shem called.

Polak held his ground and repeated the question.

Voices yelled: 'You're kidding—you're kidding!'

Suddenly Polak stepped inside, his hand over his eye.

Shem laughed. 'I tell you once, I tell you twice—and look what happens!'

There was drumming on the gates that echoed through the hollow building, while the Bullman boys howled derisively: 'Let down the rope! We'll bloody show you! Let down the rope. You scared, or what?'

Es flushed with fury. He shoved past Polak and, holding the door ajar, thrust out his head and shoulders, ready to dart back. His voice was tight and high with desperation.

'It was Red did it! It was Red broke his leg with an iron bar. You've got to help. He's got to get to hospital.'

One of the Bullman lads called back: 'Good old Red! And you folks can stay where you are. We're not letting you out. So there!'

Es flushed a darker red. 'You swine!' he shrieked.

He picked up a stone and flung it down into their midst, immediately slamming the door to. Then he stood facing his friends, gasping and sobbing with frustration, tangled curls flopping over his face, lashes glistening with tears.

George, who had been peeping through the window, said: 'You hit one of them slap on the snout.'

'Good!' cried Es, recovering with a gulp.

'Bad,' said Polak coldly. 'We needed them to help get him out before dark.'

'Oh, Christ, not another night!' George exclaimed.

'Red isn't there,' said Es at the window.

Polak spoke sharply. 'He'd better not be. Come on, George, you take Es back to the front room and Shem and me'll see what we can do with the lads. It's a matter of talking them round.'

Shem made a wry face. Es slunk by with the expression of a whipped dog. Yet he was eager to retail the bad news to Lucy and Christopher.

'Polak'll talk them round,' he added by way of consolation.

'That's no good,' Lucy said. 'Someone must go for help. If an ambulance can't get through—well—firemen must come and break down the doors. It's nonsense—police—anything!'

'Trouble is,' George explained, scratching a chilblain, 'anyone going outside now will be taken prisoner by the Bullman lads. It's part of the game, you see.'

Lucy stared and expostulated: 'But—but I mean this isn't a joke.'

'Nor is their game,' Christopher commented.

There was silence.

Lucy stood up and cried: 'Then I'll go myself. Just let them try to stop me!' She faced them, her eyes flaming.

George stopped scratching, pushed out his bottom lip and shook his head warningly at Christopher.

Christopher poked his sister in the leg. 'Hey, Lu, I won't have it. All kinds of things come into this. You don't know the lie of the land, do you? You'll go and fall down one of the old shafts Es is always telling us about. And then what help will you be? Nothing but a damned nuisance. It's not so easy in the snow. Besides that, these boys are trespassing. We don't want to see them in the courts.'

'Man, are you practical!' George broke out, admiring and mocking at the same time.

Christopher winked and then tugged his sister down till her face was almost level with his. He looked her in the eyes, passing some message the boys could not comprehend. Lucy raised one eyebrow and her forehead crinkled. She pressed his arm and sat quiet.

After a while Polak and Shem returned.

'No go,' Shem said.

Polak was ashamed to have failed. Besides, he was anxious at not being able to return home that night as expected. Es's family might go to the police.

Lucy would have liked to console Polak, seeing his square, tense shoulders shift irritably, seeing him rub at the bruise darkening his eye, seeing him shake his haystack hair.

'Never mind. We're all tired,' she said. 'How about more tea, Shem?'

Christopher was twitching and shifting with pain. Darkness shut them in.

Shem suddenly recovered. 'Lucky thing we have all this snow to boil. No snow—no tea. They'll soon be fed up and shift off home. I mean, they've no proper fire to sit round, no kettle, no home comforts, no George, no Fleabag, no nothing!'

There was a rattle at the door handle and Es let in the cat. His fur stood up specked and glistening with snow. Tail erect, he walked to the hearth and sat down. He stretched out his back leg, spread his toes and licked between each one.

George remarked: 'The most accomplished puss that ever caught a rat or sat on the hearth. In Egypt they mummified cats with best quality spices and unctions, just like they used for the Pharaohs.'

Shem turned to Christopher. 'Like a cup of char?'

Christopher smiled wanly. 'Thanks, mate.'

16

So with nothing better to do, Polak finished his story.

'The old witch—she had set her heart on murder. It's a funny thing about witches, they burn in their bellies when they want to do something that bad. Now, when you come to fairies—they don't care. They won't do their nut just because a spell fizzles out like—like a damp firework: they're maybe a bit fed up, nowt more.'

Polak's angry expression changed as soon as he began to speak. His left fist was clasped in his right hand and he sat bent towards the fire, casting up his grey eyes and concentrating inwardly, with light coming and going on his pale face and hair.

'So that night when—after Ivan passed down stream in the boat, the old girl stretches a net across the river, right from one bank to the other, and then she sits herself down in a bush to wait.'

Christopher gave a sharp grunt and clutched his thigh. 'I suppose,' Christopher gasped, 'this is how it was in the old days of witches, before morphia.'

'Shall I stop?'

'No—no, go on. It's best.'

'So the witch sits there in her bush, and the wind rushes

up river in great gusts, and she shakes with cold. She's that cold outside, but she's burning in her belly. So last thing, just before dawn breaks, here comes Ivan rowing up stream. The wind behind, giving a good push, he drives the boat slap into the net. Then it's a fine old tangle: oars stuck in the mesh, rowlocks dragged out, front all hooked up. The witch rushes out like a cat on a mouse, wades into the water and gives a big tug. The stick she fixed the net to on the far bank comes loose, the boat turns head over heels and out tumbles Ivan, with all his fishes on top of him, out into the cold river. He's one of these big lads, and his boots fill with water so he can't swim, and the net catches him and drags him under. And the witch goes on tugging till he sinks down and he's drowned dead.'

He paused to give weight to the disaster. Es stared with his mouth and eyes wide open in horror. Lucy also stared, fascinated. George and Shem listened with familiar comfort, while Christopher, propped up, twisting his beard, watched the flames and the boys alternatively. He half smiled seeing the face Es made.

'Then she hauls in the net, picks up a few fishes to put in the larder and gives Ivan a shove that sends him back into mid-stream. After this she sets the boat right and bales it out. She lays back the net and rows on to Ivan's *buda*—his—you know—his hut. She goes straight up to the door and knocks twice. And what do you think that silly dolt of a girl does? She opens up! Then the net is over her head and round her arms and she can't escape. She's dragged screaming to the shore and thrown down in bottom of the boat. And as they float down stream the sun comes up bright and shining and the witch sings out——' Polak stopped to translate in his mind. 'She sings out:

'"There's nets to—to catch fishes,
     There's nets to catch men,

And you'll be my slave
For the rest of your life.'''

There was silence.

'Is that—is that all?' Es demanded.

'What more do you want?' Polak retorted.

Es grew indignant. 'Well, I mean, his sister didn't wait for five knocks like he told her.'

Christopher said: 'Exactly. That's what comes to silly girls who don't do what their brothers say.'

Shem grinned. 'There's one for you, Lucy.'

George explained: 'She was a bit simple like, Es.'

'That's a terrible story,' Lucy said.

'And the moral?' Christopher asked.

'Moral? Oh ay, moral. Well, you might say it was—don't deny witches.' Polak looked round for approbation, feeling he might have made a joke.

Es began to hum the tune of 'Holy Night' under his breath and rock back and forth.

Christopher screwed up his face. 'I hate to think of that lovely hospital bed waiting for me. Just listen to those hooligans!'

There was the sound of abusive shouts outside.

Shem said: 'My sister Lil was given one of them jars of bath salts by a boy friend on Friday. Mauve they were—lovely colour, lovely jar, lovely bit of mauve ribbon round the top.'

Christopher chanted: 'Mauve as bridesmaids' frocks, with artificial violets smelling at the waist.'

'It's a mauve world they live in,' George responded.

'She stank the bathroom out and all.'

'You mean it stank of violets?' Es asked.

Shem made a distasteful face. 'Sort of violets. It's a funny thing about my sister Lil—she won't let anyone kiss her. They might find out she has false teeth, and her only fifteen.'

There was laughter.

Lucy said: 'I didn't realize you were a poet.'

'What, me?' Shem cried with indignation.

'No, him.' She nodded towards George.

George answered with soft earnestness, holding his head on one side, a habit that made some people wish to help him and others to hit him. 'Nay, I'm no poet, Lucy. But I tell you what, I wouldn't mind being a reporter. I'd like to be a journalist, as I was telling your brother here.' He bit a finger nail. 'I'm always asking myself, will I make it or not?'

'Why not?' Christopher demanded irritably.

'With my rotten education? In school they think we don't know, but it's plain to any fool. It's they're the daft fools thinking we don't know. That's what I say. Look at our Polak here—he'll finish up in the pits whatever his hopes may be right now.'

'You must read, George, books and books,' Christopher advised. 'You should skip school, walk into the local library and don't ever stop reading. That's the way to do it.'

'Don't be so silly!' Lucy exclaimed. 'How can he skip school, poor kid. The inspectors would be after him.'

Polak slipped off the tea chest. 'Come on, Shem. We'd best inspect. I've a feeling they're gone.'

While they were away, Lucy and Es examined the food supply and made the fire blaze. George took his account book from the desk and, after some hesitation, handed it to Christopher, saying with anxious pride:

'You know what I wrote yesterday? Would you look it over? I don't mind if you criticize—I'd be thankful. There's not many I'd take it from, if you know what I mean.'

'I don't think you'd take it even from me,' Christopher said with a grin.

He began to read, but soon the effort was too much. He laid the book on his stomach and with a sigh closed his eyes.

Lucy felt his forehead, his pulse and then whispered to George: 'We have to get him out somehow.'

George turned away, offended. He stood cracking his knuckles.

'Don't do that!' Lucy exclaimed irritably. She added: 'Has your hospital a decent reputation for orthopaedics?'

George did not reply.

Es crouched before the fire, pushing small pieces of shale through the bars. 'Lovely clean sheets they have, and dinner's not too bad, so my Mum says.' He sucked the finger he had just burnt. 'Shitty little bits of coal, these!'

'You're the only one who swears,' Lucy said. 'I've noticed.'

Es tried to explain. 'With folk you don't know you start off ever so polite. Then when you get to know them you swear and curse. It's like with the family. You wouldn't lose your wick and curse if the Queen came to tea.'

'Do you intend that as a compliment to me, or not?' Lucy smiled.

Polak and Shem came in with a gust of freezing air.

Polak commanded: 'You, George and Es, we want you below. Best take that candle end. Got the matches, George?' And he led his troops out.

As soon as she was alone with her brother Lucy again squatted beside him.

'How are you?'

'Managing.'

'What should we do?'

'If only I could get to hospital.'

'I know—I know.'

They sat quiet. The room was dark, for the shale now burnt dim and slow.

'Aren't they a rum lot?'

'I think they're marvellous.'

'So you keep telling me.'

'No—they're magnificent. Tomorrow they'll get us through anyway.'

'I'm not worried.'

'But your leg——'

'It's no use moaning, there's nothing to be done.'

They heard a thump.

Lucy hugged her knees to her chin. 'I expect their families will wonder what's happened. Isn't Es beautiful? Like a cherub that needs a scrub. And Shem is a gargoyle, and George a real live scarecrow, and Polak—as for Polak he's—he's——'

'Polak loves you.'

Lucy smiled to herself. 'I rather love Polak too. He's a leader. You don't often meet leaders of men.'

'You're just a soppy girl.'

'No, a romantic.'

'Same thing only different.'

'Are you warm?'

'For God's sake! You keep asking. Don't fuss.'

So they were quiet. Wood creaked in the roof under the weight of snow. A rat scuffled persistently under the floor. Wind slashed outside and a heavy puff of smoke bumbled out of the fireplace with a smell of soot. More thuds sounded.

At last Lucy spoke again. 'If I played my guitar in the dark it would be as though I was blind. Blindness must mean hearing and smelling and touching become new exquisite sensations. But it's broken—we might as well burn it.'

She waited for her brother's response and heard him breathe regularly. He was asleep.

17

As a last resort Polak had decided to try George's battering-ram idea. The ram they used was a scaffold pole, with two boys on each side running full tilt at the wicket door set in the big gates.

The first time George stumbled, so that they came to a jagged halt before the metal touched the wood. Next time the rod struck the cross board.

Es yelled: 'Ow—my hand!'

'Again—again!' Polak insisted. 'Run together: one-two, one-two. Inside foot first. Are you ready? Not to hold like that, George. You screw your body like it was torture.'

'It bloody well is!' said Shem, blowing on his fingers. 'Get a move on, Es! I can't stand much more!'

'Shut your mouth! I hurt my thumb!'

'I tell you once I can't stand much more. I tell you twice, I've had my dose of the Trapp. Let them find their own way out. Who invited them anyway?'

George said with sarcasm: 'What you call jerks from down south. What you call bloody foreigners.'

Polak did not understand, but the tone of their voices made him afraid. He stuttered with fury. 'You—you do not know the first—the—the first rule of life—of hospitality. Yes, I am also what you call a bloody foreigner too—a bloody

Pole! You lousy lot—you go and join them—the Bullman gang. They're the sort you belong to!'

'That's a stupid thing to say!' Shem exclaimed, and he dropped his end of the pole with a clang.

George and Es dared not speak.

Shem continued: 'You want to be cock of the roost, don't you, Polak? You want it all just how you say, and not how anyone else says, don't you? If a bloke don't agree with every whim and fancy of yours, you turn sour.'

Polak drew in his breath with indignation. 'I do not have whims and fancies!'

At this George gave his hoarse chuckle. It was luckily too dark for Polak to see Shem's long sardonic jaw thrust sideways and mocking eyes, or he would have hit out, for his fist was ready clenched.

Es whined: 'I'm fed up.'

Polak turned his head aside and swallowed his passion. They stood in the blackness, sensing the seething up and washing away of emotion, like a wave that had drawn to a huge head and then sucked back on itself. They stood frightened by the tension.

After a moment Polak said, struggling to sound normal: 'Come on, lads, let's have another crack.'

With the third bash, wood began to splinter, and at the fifth they all crumpled against the gates as the pole shot out through the hole it had made, with a long swish away into the snow. Through the torn plank light from outside glowed whitish grey.

Polak fetched another pole and continued bashing and levering until there was a gap large enough to clamber through, out into two feet of snow with more falling fast from the blanketed sky.

'No use tonight,' Shem remarked, staring up at the clouds.

'It's not so thick in this part,' Es encouraged them.

'We'll never manage all that way in the dark.'

'Most like finish up down Dog Hole or summat,' George agreed, watching Polak for some sign of agreement.

But Polak expressed no opinion: he could not speak. He stayed out in the biting air, his mind awash with conflicting ideas. He knew that Shem was right, that it would be impossible to carry the stretcher back to Slidden on such a night. But obstinately he wished to make the attempt, he wished to punish them and himself for the hateful words that had been spoken. Ideas about nationality pressed confusedly together in his mind. Then he heard Es whine:

'My thumb's gone all funny, George. Do you think it's out of joint?'

'Oh lummy, not another casualty!' George exclaimed.

So they went upstairs to settle in for the long night, each struggling to subdue thoughts of home and anxious parents and the warm bed that should have been his. Polak filled the kettle with snow, banked the fire, blocked the draughts and waited till they were all stretched out, before he himself lay down beside Es. They spoke in whispers, for fear of waking Christopher, who still slept with a twitching frown coming and going on his forehead.

Lucy said: 'It may seem foolish, but I do wish we knew the time. I forgot to wind my watch. It feels like three in the morning, yet I bet it's only somewhere round midnight. One longs to know exactly how many hours before daylight.'

Shem replied: 'You'll be lucky if it's after half ten, girl. Not having a ticker learns you to know the time.'

'Oh, God—ten hours before dawn!' She tugged the sleeping sack over her head.

Es moaned softly, 'I'm bloody cold', and almost immediately fell asleep.

Soon George was snoring intermittently, with Shem muttering, 'Pack it up, George!' every so often and kicking. Then the noise stopped, though not for long.

Restless, Lucy stretched one arm above Es's curled body.

114

Polak saw the pale shape of her hand beside his shoulder. He shifted and took the fingers within his own. They were cold and soft and so near his nose he could smell the sharp aroma of coal she had put on the fire. He smiled and wondered whether she knew who was holding her hand. Perhaps she imagined it was Es, for there was no recoil, no reaction at all. He lay quiet, and then began to smooth the back, stroking each finger that felt like a stick with bark newly peeled; he pressed the loose skin on each knuckle. The hand still lay passive, so he brought his face near and kissed the thumb. He began to believe that she must be sleeping. He kissed the palm. Then fingers stretched in a friendly curve round his face and began to feel his mouth, his cheekbone, his soft eyelid and eyebrow.

At first Polak was taken aback by the bold manner in which Lucy's hand explored, then he grew excited. He bit her thumb. This was going too far, for the arm pulled back. But he retained the wrist as firmly as he dared and suddenly, beneath his thumb, felt the pulse of blood, a tiny ripple up and down under the skin.

He lay content and the thought came to his mind: 'I shall never be so happy again.'

The hand lay against his cheek. The fire flickered orange, sending shapes up and down the walls, across the ceiling, shrinking and lengthening with sudden agility. Polak almost slept.

Except for Es, they were all roused by Christopher's groan, the hiss he gave as he drew breath between his teeth. Lucy rose to light the stump of candle. She tried to comfort him.

'Listen—the boys have broken through the gate. So the minute it's light we'll go, we'll take you to hospital. Do you understand what I'm saying?'

'Of course!' he muttered impatiently. He drew his lips back from his gums in an awful grimace.

'How can we make him easier, Lucy?' Shem asked. His conscience smote him for having suggested they should desert the brother and sister. 'How about this blanket?'

Lucy gazed back gratefully, her eyes bright in the candle-light. 'That's kind of you. Are you cold—Christopher, are you cold?'

'Of course I am!'

'If you ask me, we'd best have a cuppa,' Shem said, rising stiffly and handing Lucy his blanket.

'Would he like this one?' Polak offered, ashamed that he had not thought of the sacrifice first.

Lucy smiled. 'No—Es needs it. See the way he's curled up like a foetus! He looks sweet biting his thumb.' Her eyes met Polak's and he flushed.

The old tea leaves thrown on the fire hissed; the candle flickered down in a pool of grease on the mantelpiece; the new tea came strong and sweet.

'Pity you forgot the milk, George,' Shem remarked. He was feeling lively. 'Lucy would have loved a drop, wouldn't you, Lucy love?'

'Pity you forgot the cards,' George retorted.

Polak went out of the room into the freezing dark to drag up another plank, for wood was low again. It was easier now, because there was space for leverage, but the pitch dark was a handicap. Yet Polak felt so buoyed by the excitement of love, nothing seemed impossible, and he worked with inspired precision, as though he had been blind all his life. His hands were sore from the battering ram, blistered, his back ached, and still these discomforts were as nothing.

When he reappeared with a supply of fuel, Christopher was moaning again. Lucy sat beside her brother.

'Has it stopped snowing?' she asked.

'Just about.'

'When will it be light?'

'Three hours hence.'

116

'Is that what your biological clock says too?' she asked Shem.

'Aye—about that.'

Christopher sighed: 'I never knew a night so long.'

'There's your title for a song,' George said.

Lucy hummed on a soft husky note: 'I never knew a night so long.'

Es sat up. 'My stomach has a biological pain.'

'How long will his leg take to mend?' George asked.

'One doesn't know until one sees the X-ray.'

'What'll they do?' Es asked with relish. 'Will they operate? Will they cut it off?'

'Give over!' Shem exclaimed. 'I'm sensitive, don't you know? We're all the same in my family—sensitive.'

George remarked with contempt: 'It's always easy to be sensitive about yourself, lad.'

'Aye, some of us thrive on it!'

Lucy ignored them. 'They'll X-ray his leg, Es. Then they'll give him an anaesthetic and set the leg and put it in plaster, I expect. And then he'll have to wait around until the bone joins up.'

'Supposing it doesn't?'

Shem exclaimed impatiently: 'I wouldn't go to one of them places, not for a win on the pools!'

'I bet you would for a million pounds!' cried Es.

George said: 'My uncle broke his arm and they had to re-set it three times—you know, break the bone and start from scratch, as you might say. Worst luck it was his right arm, and he a left-handed man.'

'Specially with the strap,' Shem said.

Lucy demanded in astonishment: 'Do you mean to say he beats you?'

George replied with bitter acceptance: 'He does that.'

Lucy drew in her breath for indignant speech. 'It's disgusting—degraded!' Then she saw Polak glance up from the fire and fix his eyes on her. 'Well, I don't know, perhaps we lead a sheltered, shabby, middle-class life in London.' She put her fingers over her mouth and smiled at Polak. 'What's that scratching? It's been coming and going all night.'

Polak was considering the snow. 'We'd be OK if we had a shovel. That? Why, that's rats. They've woken up with the warm. They don't make much row this weather—you should hear them in the summer!'

18

At seven o'clock light began to seep into the gloom. Clouds hung heavily, so that the eastern sky was no brighter than the rest. A grey glow pressed listlessly into the front room.

Stiff, tired and cold, the boys stumbled about preparing for the journey. They tugged at their boots, made tea and devoured the remains of food.

'It'll be just too bad when we can't get through and have to come back,' Shem said. 'It'll mean death by starvation, I'd say.'

'You shut up!' cried Es.

The household was packed.

George hid the cups in his pocket and took the kettle in his hand, saying: 'It'd be daft to leave this for them. They'll swarm over the place like a pack of wolves once we're gone. Nothing's sacred to them!'

'We'll be in time for school, won't we?' Es asked anxiously.

Polak went out and cut the rope from the pulley. He returned winding it over his elbow and said apologetically: 'I thought this might come in on the way.' Really he intended to keep the rope for himself and had already planned where to hide it at home. He hung the loop over his shoulder.

George pocketed the accounts book, while Es tipped the remains of the coal out of the bucket, lined it with newspaper and put Polak's bed covers inside. Lucy shouldered one rucksack, George the other, while Shem and Polak lifted the stretcher on which Christopher lay pale and silent.

Coming out last, Lucy glanced back at the front room: the floor strewn with paper, empty baked bean tins, ashes, cigarette ends, the teapot on its side, the sawn-off desk, and in the corner the broken guitar, which no one could bear to burn. The deserted room was numb. She imagined how they might have to return to this desolation if it proved impossible to get through the snow. She dismissed the thought quickly.

Boots were stamping on the hollow stair, voices advising. Shem's sarcastic laugh rang out.

'Training for an ambulance man, that's me! Hold on there—I'm jammed in the corner.'

'Hey—hey!' Christopher cried as the stretcher jerked.

'Sorry, mate! You'll be OK once we're into the straight.'

They staggered on into the workshop, where snow gleamed hopefully through the smashed wicket.

Es squeezed out first and sank.

'It's up to my knees!' he shouted. 'It's in my boots! Hand over the baggage, George.'

So the rucksacks and the coal scuttle were tugged and shoved between the splintered boards.

Polak, seeing the depth of snow, looked serious and fetched part of a plank, which he ordered the unwilling George to carry. Then the stretcher was edged through, with a yell from Christopher as his leg caught on the side.

As usual Polak gave the marching orders. 'George first, then Lucy, then Es. Don't leave that plank, George, and stamp out the path as you go.'

'What we want is a sledge,' Es said.

They started off beside the mill. The new snow was soft and deep, so that they were forced to lift their feet high with every step. Scurries of wind blew down each neck, bent under its burden. The only tree, a sycamore near the stack, was a grey silhouette through the mist, its branches lined with white.

Soon Shem said: 'George'll have to take a turn. My arm's aching something cruel. Hey, you, come back out of that fog, George! You've got to take my end.'

George stood like a ghost in the distance, gazing about for landmarks.

'I was wondering which way,' he said, retracing his steps. 'You can't see a thing out there. It's like a disappearing act.'

Polak advised: 'Keep the old tumbled wall on your right, Shem. It's longer round, but we're safe that way. There's Dog Hole somewhere about.'

'I know—I know.'

Lucy stamped her feet. 'Try not to be too long. I'll take your end, Polak.'

'Nay, wait a bit till we're safe on the road. Then maybe we can go double.'

Shem walked forward with the plank. He could not see the wall through the mist. He fell into a drift. Es put down the bucket and helped him out. He moved forward, puzzled, and climbed an unfamiliar hummock. The wind blew fog about in thick masses. The Trapp was out of sight.

'Is it left?' Lucy asked anxiously.

'I keep telling him left,' Es whined.

'You don't want to come round in a circle,' Shem said. 'It's easy done.'

They plodded on, isolated from every familiar landmark. Underfoot the ground felt boggy, and not firm like the path on which they should have been walking.

Lucy thought: 'We can always go back. At least it isn't snowing. Perhaps we'd better go back. I was a fool to let them start. I should have sent Polak for help. They're only little boys. It looks like more snow. If it snows we're done for.'

She stopped and sank. The snow crumbled away as she struggled to find a firm footing.

'Plank!' yelled Polak. 'Bring that plank, Shem!'

'Rope!' yelled George. 'Chuck her the rope!'

They dumped the stretcher and Polak threw the rope to Lucy, who was sinking more slowly now, for her rucksack acted as a drag against the snow. Shem laid the plank over the abyss. She was down to her shoulders.

They dragged Lucy out, powdered white, her face pinched with alarm.

'Looks like our Lucy located Dog Hole,' Shem remarked. 'Couldn't be any other—or could it?'

The lads stared about in dismay, wondering where they were.

'Do come on, or we'll never be in school on time,' Es moaned.

But the others were already resigned to "late punishment".

A gust of wind blew a flurry of snow and Lucy saw the footsteps behind them fading from sight. She raised the blanket over Christopher's face. His eyes were closed, the eyelids very blue, his cheeks sunk and white. Snow flecked his black hair.

Then Shem's voice called: 'Here's the wall. Leastways, a wall.'

A stone wall was disclosed by the rising mist. Here and there the points of smoke-blackened stones poked out of the white blanket.

Lucy pushed Polak aside and took the steel poles from him.

'Keep away from that shaft,' Polak warned her. 'Follow me.'

While they staggered along beside the wall, slowly on and on over uneven ground, snow ceased falling, and the low sun, like a pallid egg yolk, lit the moor with its musty light. A ghostly mass of trees, bordering the lane by St Chad's, could be seen in the distance. They were pollarded and the clutch of slender branches pointing straight at the sky made them look, as George said, like a row of giant broomsticks standing upside-down.

'I wish the witches would get cracking and sweep up this snow. I'm bloody sick of snow,' Es said, and tripped on a tussock.

Lucy and George panted and struggled with the stretcher, neither wishing to admit their difficulties.

Christopher groaned softly: 'Hey, if you two could keep in step——'

'Are you cold?' Lucy gasped.

'I don't know. That's nothing.'

They stopped again to exchange burdens with Shem and Polak. Polak bowed his head and began to sing:

'Wojenko, wojenko, co jest ta za pani?
Ida za toba chlopce malowane,
Chlopce malovane sami wybierane.
Wojenko, wojenko, co jest ta za pani?'

'What does that mean?' Lucy called back over her shoulder.

'It's an army song from my father. It means:

'War, war, what kind of lady are you?

After you are going painted boys——

'You know, that means painted with youth, with red cheeks.

'Painted boys all chosen.

'It means, special, specially chosen—the flower of youth—summat like that.

'War, war, what kind of lady are you?

'That's a good marching song, he always said.'

Away over the hill a Land Rover could be seen moving smoothly across the white moor, with sooty sheep gathering and following after.

'That'll be Bob Riddell,' George said. 'He's tossing out bales of hay. If only we could hail him.'

'He'd never make it across the beck.'

They stood longing for the Land Rover, then turned away and trudged on, till the ditch slanted up and through a tumbled gap to the road.

'It wasn't that bad after all,' Es said. He had a feeling of disappointment as well as relief.

Lucy spoke sharply: 'Right, Es, your go at the stretcher. One on each corner now.'

St Chad struck eight as they passed.

George, whose turn it was to rest, leapt up the churchyard bank and, standing before a sheltered gravestone, spread his arms wide. His shirt tail hung out below his jacket. He read in a sonorous voice: '"Here lies the Great Earl of Mexborough. He was descended from an Illustrious Family in this County, whose Antiquity cannot be traced."'

With a cry of rocketing, humourless laughter, he stood above the passing stretcher party. Then he broke off a chunk of black green moss and flung it as hard as he could at the church window. It fell short, driving a neat, deep hole in the snow.

19

So the boys came back to Slidden on Monday morning. They kept to the top road that led round the hillside to the hospital, in order to avoid the busy town centre. They passed the end of the street where Polak and Shem lived, and along the row of shabby shops, whose windows never changed except to grow more faded and dusty. The butcher's doorway was filled with the carcase of a pig hung upside-down, its hind hooves caught on two iron hooks that stuck out either side of the frame for this purpose. The animal's guts had been cleaned and white fat lay smooth and stretched, except where bulging globules covered the kidneys.

Frank Hall stood behind his pig and looked out between the legs at the passing cortège. He straddled, knife in hand. His red face with purple ears was going flabby.

He shouted: 'Ee—you!'

Polak ducked his head away and said to Shem: 'Go on —he won't give over till you've told him.'

Shem, now the free member of the party, went across the cobbles.

The butcher would have come out had not the carcase blocked his way. 'Who've you got here, Shem lad?'

'Bloke broke his leg. We're taking him to hospital.'

'One of our lads?'

'Nay, he's from London.'

'And where have you been all week-end? Your young sister was sent up to ask.'

Shem edged back. 'We've not been far—not far,' he said. 'Once we've dumped him——' He paused and changed his mind. 'We're taking him to hospital.' He stepped into the road.

'Don't you try and bluff me, lad!' Frank Hall shouted in his ringing bass for all the street to hear. 'They'll give you six of the best when you get to school!'

Shem fled after his friends, who were scurrying to avoid further interference. Only the sight of the hospital slowed them down.

Es asked Lucy: 'Will they cut his hair and shave off his beard?'

Lucy saw the stone Gothic porch, round which was carved in serifed letters, 'Slidden Voluntary Hospital'.

'I expect Casualty is round the corner somewhere.'

'Nay, everyone goes in this door,' Es replied.

'Is my face as dirty as yours?' Lucy asked.

'Not at all!' Polak said.

The others laughed.

Lucy smoothed her hair and held the door for them to enter. Inside they laid the stretcher on the stone flags and stood rubbing their aching arms.

The porter, lurking in a glass box, leant forward and called out angrily: 'Don't dump it in the middle of the passage. Put it up on that there trolley.'

Lucy stepped forward and spoke with her most authoritative London accent. The boys crowded round to see how the official would respond. A woman in a big blue skirt, with white starched sleeves and a frilled cap trotted down the passage. Lucy immediately turned, her voice sweet and soothing.

'I'm afraid he's rather cold, sister,' she apologized. 'We've come in from the moor.'

126

'Take him up to ward three, Mason,' the sister ordered.

'Best of luck, Christopher!'

Christopher's stiff grey face moved. 'Bye—and thanks!' He spoke very quietly.

'Where will I find you?' Lucy asked the boys, her eyes on the moving trolley.

Polak replied: 'The caff off March Street. Jim's caff it's called. Anyone'll tell you. We'll leave your gear here. Right?'

'I'll bring your blankets,' she said. 'I must go.' She was going. Long legs and bounding hair gone up the passage and round the corner.

They stood disconsolate.

Shem said: 'Nine twenty-five—no sense in going to school now. It'll only mean trouble. No sense in asking for trouble.'

They left the rucksack in the porter's box and trailed out into Slidden with nothing to do.

'You'd best run off home, Es, or they'll have the coppers after you.'

'You're telling me! My Mum'll be doing her nut.'

George told him: 'All you have to say is—you went out to the Trapp Sunday afternoon. Right? Don't mention Saturday. Right? So we were besieged by the Bullman Lane lads. Got it? And then there was this fellow had his leg broke. So you had to stay on and help. Right? Just tell the truth, but not too much.'

Es nodded sadly. He had no wish to leave his friends, to plunge into rows, explanations, punishments.'

'And get your face washed!' Polak said, giving him a push.

The three older ones went down a steep alley into the town. The purposelessness of life after the weekend weighed on their spirits. They kicked the snow and hung their heads and slithered, unmindful of the world.

George asked: 'Think Jim'll stand us a cup of tea?'

'You're kidding,' Shem retorted.

'I'll fix it,' Polak said.

Shem looked at him. 'You're a right miser! So you kept a bit of money back.'

He shoved Polak and they began to run, gasping and slipping and bumping against each other, with George trailing behind at an uneven trot. The snow grew browner and wetter as they descended. Buses and cars spurted slush at them in the main street. The squelching and the roaring vibration of engines jarred after the silence of the moor.

Jim's Café stood in a dilapidated, cobbled yard. Its windows were steamed up, but through them the electric light glowed hazily. The glass in the door rattled as Shem turned the handle, and there was the familiar, cosy, dirty room. The walls were decorated with old advertisements: the Pepsi-Cola squiggle, the bearded sailor from Player's cigarettes stained yellow with foul nicotine air. On the counter ranged a formation of white cups upside-down, the urn glowed musty silver. Yesterday's cigarette ends and paper littered the floor. On a table stood a new brown boot. In the gloom at the far end, where Jim would not turn on the light unless asked, lurked the fruit machine and the one-armed bandit. There was a dank chill to the place.

As soon as George sat down he became aware of his feet: of their wet cold agony. He stood up, unable to bear the throbbing chilblains, and called huskily through to the back.

'Shop!'

Jim could be heard thumping downstairs unevenly, for one leg was shorter than the other. He entered puffing and affected astonishment.

'What are you bad lads doing here of a Monday morning?'

His forehead protruded like a huge grey pebble smoothed on the seashore, his eyes popped like blue and white marbles

128

about to drop out, while the rest of his face and greasy chin sloped steadily down into a fat neck.

'Three teas, Jim,' George said.

'Sure you can afford it?' Jim asked, staring meaningfully at Shem, who owed him five pence.

Polak produced the money. Jim laid the change on top of the till.

'That's a new calendar you got there,' Shem remarked to show he was not worried about his debt. 'What you might call gorgeous.'

All except Jim, who was bent before the urn, looked at the wall behind the counter where a big coloured picture, unsullied and fresh, revealed 'January Ginger'. She was a young lady with red curls falling about her shoulders, a soft, coy smile, and nothing to hide her warm nakedness but carefully placed soap bubbles.

George considered: 'They must make them bubbles with washing-up liquid, don't you think? Powder makes a much tighter type of foam.'

'You should try experimenting on your girl friend,' Jim said.

Shem smirked: 'I wonder what Miss Lucy would say if we asked her to try experimenting.'

George grinned and looked towards Polak, who flushed, opened his mouth, almost spoke, and then shut it tight, glaring at the counter.

Shem mocked: 'I'd clean forgotten—our Polak doesn't like "whims and fancies".'

'Tea up!' cried Jim.

While they drank Polak would not speak. He felt humiliated at having given himself away.

George kept yawning and closing his eyes between drinks.

'It's my back as aches worst.' He mouthed a silent sentence and then continued: 'They were both broken when I came to look. It was Lucy tumbling into Dog Hole. I must have knocked them with that plank you would have me carry. It was a rotten shame. Both of them.'

'Oh—you mean them cups you nicked?' Shem said. He rose self-consciously and carried his cup back to the counter.

'I'll be going,' he said, and saw the change on top of the till.

'That belongs to your friend,' Jim told Shem.

Shem took the coin, spun it in the air, and clapped his hands together. He opened them and affected surprise. 'Look at that—tails! Sorry—you lose, Polak. I'll have a go. Remember the other week when I won the jackpot? Turn up the light, Jim.'

He went to the alcove and George followed.

On the glass front of the fruit machine were painted girls. They wore enormous hats on which numbers were marked. Sixty-eight was dressed in a pink crinoline with a strapless bodice and a black ribbon round the neck. On her arms were long green gloves and a vast expanse of underarm showed as she waved a heart at customers. Forty wore a blue hat and had silver stars on her black crinoline: she carried a watering-can. The ladies behind had laughing mouths and equine teeth.

'Egg and chips,' cried Shem. 'Come on, sweetheart, cough up egg and chips all round!'

The box instructed: 'When magic lines are lit move levers indicated. Lucky pockets. Gay time games. Tons of fun.'

Shem pushed the coin. Knobs lit, green—red—blue, bells tinkled in the upper region. Shem pulled the levers deftly and each gave a hiccup as he did so. Then from the bowels of the machine there came an ominous clang. He pulled another lever, but it no longer responded. The lights went out. Shem pulled again. It was dead. He took the sides of the box and shook it angrily. It only shivered and tinkled with faint protest.

Shem strode back to Polak. 'No luck today, mate. I'm off

to tell my old woman I haven't emigrated, not yet. She won't half be chuffed.'

Polak did not move or look up.

George said: 'Frank Hall will have spread that news.'

'Are you coming, George, or not?' Shem demanded.

'Aye, might as well. But—but what about her?'

Polak cut in fiercely: 'I'm staying.'

So Polak was left alone. He sat dazed and day-dreaming for some time, then rose and carried over the cups.

'Give us the brush, Jim. I'll sweep round. If you need a hand with the washing up dinner time I've nothing special on.'

'And why aren't you lads at school, pray?' Jim asked, coming out of his own dreams across the counter and handing over the broom.

'We had a bit of a dust up with Bullman Lane lads last night, over at Trapp's Mill. This London bloke broke his leg and we couldn't fetch him back, what with snow and all, not till this morning. We brought him along to hospital.'

He piled the chairs on the tables with swift professionalism and swept.

Jim watched, elbows on the counter. 'So you've been sleeping over at Trapp's.' He enjoyed Polak's efficiency with the broom. 'These days, you young ones, you don't know what you want. When I was your age you got a job and you had to lump it or like it.' He nodded his head at his own wisdom. 'Aye—and what's this bird you're waiting on? Miss Lucy.'

Polak swept in a corner, his head down. 'She's his sister. Who's this old boot belong to? It's bad luck to put it on the table.'

Jim made a dour face. 'Is that so? Last night a one-legged Irish tramp comes in, and when he's had his cup of tea and bread and marg, he gets up holding this boot. So he goes to the door and he says, says he, "This article is off me other leg, the one you've never met. But", says he, "I'm leavin' it with you in case me other half drops in some time." And with that he lays it on the table and skips off into the snow without paying a penny.'

Polak smiled to think of Jim's slovenly indolence, his inability to chase even a one-legged tramp for his money.

The door gave its grating shudder and Lucy entered, her arms piled with the blankets and quilt, her nose pink.

'How is he?' Polak asked, taking the bedclothes.

She smiled. 'Not too bad, I hope. Es'll be disappointed. They aren't cutting it off.'

'I was just thinking this boot would have served him. It'll have to wait for another customer, won't it, Jim? What'll you have now?'

'Let's have——' She gazed at Polak, smiling. 'I expect you're hungry. Let's have—two teas and two eggs and chips twice.'

They sat waiting.

'How will you manage?' Polak asked.

'I phoned my father's office. He's coming up tonight by car, and then we can take Christopher down. His leg will be in plaster.'

The thought of parting made them unable to look at each other.

At last Polak said in a strained voice: 'You won't forget the Trapp, will you?'

Lucy shook her head. 'No, I won't.'

Their eyes met, and then both looked away, unable to bear it.

So they sat with nothing more to say.